VEX

INTERGALACTIC DATING AGENCY

DRAGON BRIDES
BOOK 12

KATE RUDOLPH

He's fire and fury. She's the lie that could cost him everything.

Dragon Lord Vex doesn't lose control. Ruthless, disciplined, and sworn to the crown, he's the king's deadliest operative and he has no patience for distractions.

Until Luisa.

She's sharp-tongued, brilliant, and completely off-limits. But to infiltrate a criminal syndicate stealing elite identities from the Intergalactic Dating Agency, Vex has to pretend she's his mistress.

Fake chemistry? No problem.

But it doesn't feel fake.

The heat between them is undeniable. But Luisa's hiding dangerous secrets, and when Vex uncovers the truth, it shatters more than their mission.

Her betrayal cuts deeper than any blade.

His silence hurts more than frostbite.

And the enemy is watching… ready to strike.

With a deadly network closing in, their only hope is each other. But can a dragon who lives by duty risk everything for a woman who breaks all the rules?

One grumpy dragon lord. One secretive human heroine. A fake relationship with scorching consequences.

1

HIS BROTHER WAS GOING to get himself killed.

Lord Vex stalked back and forth across the room and grit his teeth. A wisp of smoke came off of his shoulders, which only made him more frustrated. That lack of control was emblematic of some fledgling, not a dragon warrior of Vemion.

If he left today, he could be on Earth in a week.

Would Rook already be dead?

His last call had left Vex, well, vexed.

What in all of the stars could have induced his brother to walk into a situation like that without backup?

That settled it. He was going.

Vex yanked open the armored cabinet beside

his bed, the biometric lock recognizing his finger-print with a soft chime. His field kit was already assembled: backup power cells, currency chips, tactical armor folded into a compression pack no larger than his fist. He grabbed his travel bag from the closet and began shoving items inside with military efficiency. Extra clothes, his personal sidearm, the diplomatic credentials that would get him through jump gates without questions.

He paused, holding a formal dress jacket. When had he become the brother who dropped every-thing to chase after the others? Rook was a grown dragon. A lord of Vemion. He could handle himself.

The jacket went into the bag anyway.

His communicator buzzed against the night-stand. Vex lunged for it, hoping for word from his brother, but the display showed only routine fleet reports. Nothing from Earth. Nothing from Rook.

His butler, Orinn, stood in the doorway, and Vex stopped in his tracks. His own expression was bland, he knew, but he'd torn up half the room looking for his things rather than calling a servant to do the job.

This was not like him.

He didn't like to worry.

If Rook survived, Vex was going to kill him.

Orinn's weathered face remained perfectly composed, but Vex caught the slight tightening around his eyes as the butler surveyed the chaos. Drawers hung open, formal uniforms draped over chairs, and navigation charts scattered across the floor like fallen leaves. The old servant had seen Vex prepare for dozens of missions over the years, each one methodical and precise.

This was neither.

"What?" Vex demanded. It was a bit snappish.

Damn it. Damn Rook.

He straightened, running a hand through his hair. Taking it out on servants was unbecoming.

"A message from your uncle, my lord." His tone was perfectly neutral, the way it always was when delivering news that might not be welcome.

His uncle. The king. Orrin seemed to take a certain pleasure in always referencing the familial relation. The parchment was sitting on a silver tray in his hands.

Vex snatched it and read, his scowl growing deeper with each word. The parchment was expensive and thick between his fingers, the kind that crinkled softly when handled. His uncle's personal seal was pressed deep into the crimson wax, the dragon sigil catching the light.

Assistance is requested at your earliest convenience.

Then there was an address. Nothing else.

His uncle did like to be brief.

Vex looked up to find Orinn watching him with that patient expression that meant there was more coming. The butler's hands were clasped behind his back now, the silver tray tucked under one arm.

The butler cleared his throat. "There was also a message from your brother, sir."

Vex's grip tightened on the parchment. "Which brother?" he snapped.

The one on the suicide mission or the one who wouldn't know responsibility if he was chained to it?

"Lord Rook, sir." Orinn's voice remained steady, but his gaze flicked toward the scattered belongings on the floor. "He is on his way home." The butler's expression flickered, just for an instant, like a man who'd tasted something sour and was trying not to show it.

"What is it?"

Orinn straightened his shoulders, as if bracing for impact. "He's bringing his mate. And he invites you to dinner."

The words hung in the air between them. Vex felt his jaw clench, the familiar heat building in his chest. Smoke curled from his nostrils without his permission.

"His mate," Vex repeated slowly.

"Yes, my lord."

"The brother who was supposed to be on a simple retrieval mission to Earth has found his mate."

"It would appear so, my lord."

Vex was going to kill Rook.

He looked at the mess of his rooms. It looked like a whirlwind had torn through the space, leaving chaos in its wake. Then he looked back at his butler, who was watching him with the resigned patience of someone who had witnessed many family crises over the years.

"Very well." Vex's voice was clipped, controlled. "Send him my regards."

Orinn inclined his head. "Shall I convey any particular sentiment, my lord?"

The question was asked so blandly that Vex almost smiled despite his frustration. Almost.

"Tell him I look forward to meeting his mate," Vex said. "And that I'm pleased he's returned safely."

It was better to let the butler do it. If Vex sent his own message full of his actual feelings and the curses to back them up, Rook might never come back to Vemion.

Orinn moved toward the door, then paused. "Shall I have the household prepare for your departure, my lord?" Departure was what usually followed a message from the king.

Vex carefully folded the parchment in hand. "Yes."

"Very good, sir." Orinn hesitated for just a moment. "If I may, my lord, Lord Rook has always been remarkably adept at landing on his feet."

The comment was offered quietly, but Vex caught the gentle reassurance in it. His butler had watched all three brothers grow up. He knew them better than most.

"Thank you, Orinn."

The butler bowed and withdrew, leaving Vex alone with the royal summons and his scattered belongings.

At least he was no longer torn between his duty to save his brother and his duty to the king.

An hour later, he was walking up the high street, trying not to wonder what the king wanted him to do. King Venin was family, but he was still a king.

And he had no qualms using Vex's skills, no matter what kind of danger that put Vex in.

Vex had the scars to prove it.

He really hoped there weren't any slime monsters this time. He'd lost his favorite suit on that mission.

Royal Matchmaker.

The sign on the door stopped him in his tracks.

Was his uncle setting him up? Vex supposed it might be time to find a bride of his own, but surely this was not the way to go about it.

It didn't stop him from going in. If the king wanted him there at his earliest convenience, then there he would be.

But no one was there.

The shop was all soft femininity that made Vex feel like a weapon in a jewelry box. Pale walls were adorned with watercolor paintings of flowers and romantic garden scenes, their frames curved and delicate. A low velvet couch faced two matching chairs across a polished table where he might have expected a desk. Lace curtains filtered the afternoon light into something dreamy and diffused. Crystal figurines lined the windowsill, catching the light and casting tiny rainbows across the carpet.

Everything had rounded edges, soft textures,

gentle colors. Not a single harsh line or sharp angle in sight. The air smelled of vanilla and roses.

This was definitely not designed for dragon warriors.

A voice drifted through the room, apologetic and slightly breathless. "I'm sorry, but I have an appointment." A woman in a silky blue dress came out from a room in the back.

She moved with an odd, ethereal quality, as if she was listening to something he couldn't hear. Her dark hair was pinned up in an elaborate style that somehow managed to look both elegant and slightly disheveled.

Vex held up the parchment, the royal seal visible. "I believe that would be me."

The woman stopped in her tracks, her eyes widening as they fixed on the parchment. Her shoulders dropped as if a weight had been lifted from them.

"Thank the gods." The relief in her voice was strong. She gestured toward the seating area with a graceful wave of her hand. "Please, sit. Would you like tea? I have an excellent blend from the eastern provinces."

Vex remained standing, studying her face. There was something unsettling about her gaze, but he wasn't sure what. "I'd like to know what this meeting is about."

She tilted her head, considering him for a moment before moving to one of the delicate chairs. Her movements were fluid, practiced, but there was tension in the line of her spine.

"Of course. Please, make yourself comfortable."

She took a seat in one of the chairs, and he chose the couch. The moment he sat down, the cushions seemed to swallow him. It was so soft he wished he had stayed standing.

The woman folded her hands in her lap, her posture suddenly very formal. "My name is Shade. I'm the Royal Matchmaker."

Vex shifted, trying to find a more dignified position on the overstuffed couch. "Yes. If you wanted to make a match for me, I'm not sure a royal summons was necessary."

She looked at him then, head tilted to the side, and seemed to gaze off somewhere he couldn't see. Her eyes went unfocused, almost cloudy, and for a moment, she seemed to be listening to a conversation only she could hear.

"Hmm." She blinked, shaking her head as if clearing it. When her gaze refocused on him, it was sharp and businesslike. "I need your help with a delicate situation."

Vex leaned forward slightly, his hands braced on his knees. "A lady in trouble?"

Shade's smile turned rueful. "Only if I'm the lady." She paused, seeming to weigh her words carefully. "Someone has stolen confidential data from my parent organization, the Intergalactic Dating Agency. I need you to retrieve it."

Ah.

That kind of help.

At least it didn't sound slimy.

"What do you need?" he asked, his voice taking on the clipped efficiency he used for mission briefings.

Shade's shoulders relaxed a fraction more. "The stolen data contains highly sensitive information about our clients. Names, profiles, personal details of some of the most powerful individuals in the galaxy."

"Including members of the royal family?"

"Yes," she confirmed quietly.

Vex felt his jaw tighten. No wonder his uncle had sent him personally. "Who took it?"

"A criminal syndicate operating out of Aetis."

Shade's voice carried a note of distaste. "They're using it for blackmail, extortion, and worse."

The name of the planet made Vex's stomach sink slightly. Aetis was not known for its hospitality or its law-abiding citizens.

"I see." He stood, the soft couch finally releasing him. "When do I leave?"

2

LUISA HATED WORKING WITH AMATEURS.

The message from her contact had been sparse on details, but crystal clear on one thing: she'd have a partner. A partner she'd never worked with, never vetted, never even heard of in the networks that kept track of who was competent and who got people killed.

If she'd known about the partner when the offer came through, she would have turned it down flat and walked away. It was what any self-respecting loner would do.

She scoffed. *Yeah, right.* Like rent wasn't due and her accounts weren't teetering between low and empty.

There's an easy way to fix that, a traitorous little

voice whispered in her mind. It would take nothing to fix her money problems. One computer terminal, a few clicks of the keyboard, and voilà, an unending stream of credits.

Her fingers twitched. The old hunger stirred, that electric thrill of cracking open a system and watching numbers cascade across her screen.

Luisa refused to entertain the idea. The allegedly unending stream of credits tended to end at the end of some goon's bat or in a cell. There weren't laws on Aetis, not really, but separating rich people from their money led to bad things.

Very bad things.

She'd seen what happened to thieves who were unlucky enough to steal from the wrong mark. The memory of broken fingers flashed through her mind before she could stop it.

Luisa was reformed. She didn't need to steal to make a living, not when the Intergalactic Dating Agency was out there offering a ludicrous amount of credits to someone who could retrieve their stolen data.

And that she could do.

But she hated the undercity.

The neon-slicked streets stretched out before her like a fever dream painted in electric blues and poisonous greens. Holographic advertisements flickered against crumbling concrete walls, promising everything from synthetic highs to flesh that would love you for an hour. The air tasted of desperation, thick with the exhaust from hover-bikes and the sweet cloying smell of whatever they were cooking in the food stalls.

Bodies pressed past her in the narrow alleys, some putting on elaborate fronts of wealth they didn't possess, others so beaten down by the weight of survival that they moved like ghosts. A woman in a torn sequined dress leaned against a doorway, her smile bright and brittle as she called out to potential customers. Two blocks down, a man sat slumped against a wall, and he didn't look like he'd see tomorrow.

She reached the edge of The Veil, that slim slice of the undercity clinging to respectability or clawing its way out of the muck, depending on who you asked.

Here, the streets were wider and somewhat clean. Corporate security guards in crisp uniforms stood at strategic corners, their presence a reminder that someone with money cared enough to keep the chaos at bay.

The lights were softer, more tasteful, advertising

legitimate businesses alongside the questionable ones. But the streets were nearly empty, as if the sanitized atmosphere had sucked the life out of the place along with the obvious crime.

The Veil was an illusion. Give her the grit of the undercity any day.

But Undertow didn't suck.

It was one of the seedier bars in the Veil, with digital gaming tables in the back that were always busy with patrons. The porn machines in the back room were even busier. A middle-aged man in an expensive coat emerged from that back room, his face flushed with shame but his stride carrying just a hint of swagger. He avoided eye contact with everyone as he hurried toward the exit.

The swill out of their taps was drinkable, and she'd never gotten food poisoning there. It was a good place for a first date.

She snorted.

But working with a partner was a bit like dating, and she had to feel out her amateur before they got to the show. Her contact at the IDA had been scant on the details. Dating profile data had been stolen. That data included information from high rollers across the galaxies that could be used for blackmail, or worse.

Luisa wondered what people were putting in their dating profiles that could get them blackmailed.

Then again, people were ashamed of the strangest things. She glanced back toward the porn room, where another patron was trying to look casual as he slipped inside.

The bar's interior was dimly lit, dark shadows and flickering holo-displays showing sports feeds from a dozen different worlds. Conversations buzzed at a low level, the kind of careful murmur that suggested everyone was keeping their own secrets.

Undertow was full of its usual mix of patrons, which made her contact stand out like a piece of gold in a trash dump.

He was … elegant.

Dark hair swept back from a face that belonged in a corporate boardroom or a government building, not a dive bar in the Veil. His suit was perfectly tailored, the kind of understated luxury that cost more than most people made in a year. Everything about him screamed money and breeding, from his straight posture to the way he held his hands.

Three different street thieves she recognized were already eyeing him like he was their next meal. Rory was closest, his fingers already twitching toward the knife he kept hidden in his sleeve.

If the amateur escaped with his wallet, he'd be lucky.

This job was going to suck.

Luisa marched up to the table and put herself between the amateur and Rory. "We're not talking out here," she said.

The man looked up at her and raised one perfect eyebrow. She was struck by his eyes, a deep hazel with flecks of gold in them.

Hells, even his eyes were rich.

Her pulse kicked up a notch, heat spreading through her chest in a way that had nothing to do with the stuffy bar. This was not good. This was the *opposite* of good. She was supposed to be the professional here, the one who knew how to handle herself in any situation.

No funny business on the job.

He didn't say a word or try to move.

Just sat there watching her with those impossibly composed eyes, as if he was cataloging every detail of her appearance and filing it away for later analysis. The silence stretched between them, and it was getting uncomfortable.

"Come on." Luisa nodded towards the back. "There are ears everywhere."

Still, the man said nothing.

His stillness was unnerving. Most people fidgeted when they were nervous, especially in a place like this. But he sat like a statue, perfectly controlled and calm. It was either the mark of someone with serious training or someone too naive to understand the danger he was in.

Had she called it wrong? She'd be grateful if her partner wasn't this … mark. But no one else in the room fit the bill.

"Are you interested in antiquities?" the man finally asked. His voice was low, cultured, with just a hint of an accent she couldn't place.

The goddamn password. Right.

"Only if they're alabaster," she said through gritted teeth.

The man stood. "Vex."

Yes, she was vexed.

No. That was his name.

"Luisa."

He nodded. "You said there's somewhere we can talk?"

She pointed back towards the gaming tables and porn bots.

Vex's gaze followed her gesture, taking in the flashing lights and the steady stream of patrons moving in and out of the back rooms. He looked at her, eyes flicking up and down. The assessment was clinical, professional, but she felt it like a touch. Luisa tried to ignore the way a flash of heat surged through her. There was nothing hot in his eyes.

She'd never known hazel eyes could be so cold.

"I'm here for a job," he said, "not ... that."

Nevertheless, he followed her back to the biggest porn booth. The machine was currently unoccupied, its screen cycling through advertisements for various fantasy scenarios. Naked women flashed on the screen behind them, and Luisa did her best not to touch any surfaces. Who knew when that thing got hosed down?

"Already you take me to the most interesting places," Vex murmured. There was the faintest hint of amusement in his voice.

"I can show you a world of ..." Luisa couldn't figure out how to end the sentence. Heat crept up her neck. What was wrong with her? She shook her head. Time for business. "My contact said we're going to the Mountain. That's where the info's coming out of."

The Mountain Gate Casino Resort was a

legend among Aetis's impossible venues. It was a playground for the highest of high rollers. There weren't any roads up; you arrived by air or not at all. And the minimum cost of a room was more than Luisa had in her bank account at the best of times.

Vex looked like he could afford it. But he also looked more like a scholar than a gambler.

"I was sent the dossier on our identities. Are you going to be able to pull that off?" The cover story was predictable and insulting in equal measure. Of course she had to pretend to be his arm candy. For some reason, people that were Mountain-rich never believed someone like *her* could bring in the money.

Vex gave a single nod.

Not a man of many words.

"Look, this is going to require trust," she said. She leaned closer, lowering her voice. The booth's walls were thin, and sound carried in places like this. "I have to get physical access to their system to start scanning for our intel. That means you're my shield. If they don't buy—"

"They'll buy it," Vex assured her. His voice carried absolute certainty. "This is not my first assignment."

She took in his suit, his haircut, his … everything. "So it's your second?"

That got a small smile out of him. The expression transformed his face completely, turning him from coldly handsome to devastatingly attractive. Her stomach did something complicated and entirely unprofessional. "I will trust you if you trust me. Are you ready to go?"

"What? Now?" She thought this was a meet and greet, not that she was going to run away with him.

"The sooner we start, the sooner this is all over."

The faster she could complete the job, collect her payment, and get away from her mysterious partner, the better.

On that they could agree.

3

THEY MET where the Veil met the true edge of the city two hours later. Luisa had her supplies: a backpack full of computer equipment and one change of clothes. From experience, she knew that clothes for Luisa the Mistress would be waiting for them when they arrived.

The edge of the city was crumbling to nothing. Buildings stood like broken teeth, their facades decayed and windows dark. Beyond the final row of ramshackle shelters lay nothing but empty lots scattered with rusted metal and pools of chemical runoff that gleamed with an oily sheen. Only the most desperate scraped out a living in this forgotten zone, and they rarely survived long enough to make a true home.

Vex had changed clothes. If anything, he looked *more* expensive than before. His suit's edges were crisper. It had cuff links that winked with diamonds. And there was just an air of money she couldn't quite describe.

The fabric had to cost more than her rent for a year. Every line was perfectly tailored, every detail screaming wealth so loudly it was almost vulgar. This wasn't just expensive clothing. This was armor made of credits and status.

Okay, maybe he had some idea about what he was doing.

"Where's our ride?" she asked. She'd expected some kind of sleek little transport, expensive, impractical, and perfect for their cover. And she'd already been thinking up excuses for why she should be the one to drive.

Not that she didn't trust Vex.

She just really loved sporty vehicles.

"I thought we'd make a statement," he said blandly. "You'll want to put on something warmer."

Something in the air changed. The atmosphere seemed to thicken, pressing against her eardrums until they popped. Heat shimmered around Vex like a mirage, distorting his outline. Luisa felt a shift and blinked, her ears popping. Then Vex was surrounded by light and color, and after a moment, there was a freaking *dragon* left in his place.

She scrambled back, mouth open wide. "What —how? Wha—" No one told her she was working with ... this!

Luisa knew about dragons, sure. Vemion wasn't that far, and dragon lords slummed it on Aetis from time to time. But she'd never seen one transform. She'd never thought she'd get up close to one.

Vex was gorgeous. Sleek black scales covered his massive form. Veins of gold ran through the darkness, threading across his hide. The metallic tracery followed the powerful lines of his body, highlighting the corded muscle beneath. Up close, she could make out individual scales, each one perfectly formed and fitted to its neighbors like armor.

Professional curiosity warred with something deeper. Her fingers twitched with the urge to reach out, to see if those scales were as smooth as they looked. She almost reached out but pulled her hand back.

Would he be cool with that? It seemed too personal, and she just met the man.

"Wait, are you ... are we ... do you want to fly up there with ... me?" She stared at the dragon and waited for an answer.

And waited.

Right. He wasn't going to talk when he looked like that. Did he even have vocal cords?

But she could have sworn she almost heard, or maybe it was better to say *felt,* something coming from him.

Were dragons psychic?

Yeah, no way in hell was she voicing that question.

She pulled a jacket out of her pack and hoped it would do. The Mountain was called that for a reason—it was high in a range that couldn't be undertaken by foot and full of ice and snow and all that fun stuff.

Vex extended his leg and wing to make a sort of ramp up to his back.

He wanted her to climb on.

"I don't suppose there's a saddle?" she asked.

This time, she was almost certain she felt laughter in her mind.

No saddle.

Luisa climbed on and was surprised by how sturdy the dragon was. His body was solid muscle beneath her palms, warm and impossibly strong.

At first, she felt stable, like maybe this would work.

Then Vex shifted his weight, and she nearly bucked off. She threw herself down on his back, lying flat, trying to fling her legs on either side of him and grip with her thighs like he was a giant horse. Her legs barely reached halfway around his torso.

But he was way gianter than a horse.

I won't drop you. She had to be hallucinating out of fear because that was definitely her partner's voice in her head.

And why did it sound sexy?

The mental voice carried the same controlled confidence as his speaking voice, but there was something intimate about hearing it directly in her thoughts. Heat coiled low in her stomach, completely inappropriate and utterly unwelcome.

Fear and wonder. Or something. Luisa did *not* have time for attraction.

Or hallucinations.

The ground fell away beneath them with a rush of displaced air. Wind battered her face, stealing her breath and making her eyes water. Her hands cramped from gripping his scales so tightly, but she didn't dare loosen her hold. The city shrank below them at an alarming rate.

He eventually evened out in altitude, and Luisa

started to relax a little. Curiosity finally overcame terror. She opened her eyes and gasped in wonder. From this height, even the squalor of the undercity looked almost beautiful, the neon signs creating rivers of colorful light that flowed between the buildings like magic.

But they quickly passed the city and turned for the mountains. The temperature dropped noticeably as they gained altitude, and she shivered despite her jacket. Then, as if responding to her discomfort, Vex's body temperature seemed to increase, warmth radiating through his scales like a living heating system.

Was that a dragon thing? she wondered. Or was she just imagining things again?

The view was spectacular. Jagged peaks stretched out in all directions, their snow-covered summits gleaming under the moonlight. The silence was profound, broken only by the steady rhythm of Vex's wingbeats and the whisper of wind over scales. She took in the view and relaxed some more.

It really was quite wonderful.

And just as she was beginning to think she could get used to that, Vex folded his wings and dove.

"What the hell?" It was half-shriek, half-yell.

"Are you trying to get me killed?" She clung to him tighter.

There was more of that impossible laughter in her mind.

After an hour or so, she saw the lights of the Mountain in the distance. The casino resort grew larger with startling speed, its impossible architecture becoming clear as they approached. Glass and steel jutted from the sheer rock face, defying gravity and common sense.

Vex's landing was pure showmanship, a spiraling descent that ended with a flourish of wings and a perfect touchdown on the resort's private landing pad. Her legs shook as she slid down from his back. She did her best to maintain her dignity. She was on the job now and had a part to play.

The transformation from dragon to man seemed to happen faster than the other way. One second he was the glorious black beast, the next he was … a different man entirely.

Gone was the composed, controlled professional from the bar. This version of Vex moved with a predator's agility, his smile sharp and knowing. He leered at her and swaggered, throwing his arm negligently around her shoulder. Then he leaned in and nuzzled her neck, hot breath ghosting over her skin.

The contact sent an unwelcome shiver through her. His touch was confident, possessive, and completely at odds with the reserved man she'd met hours earlier. When had Vex transformed from uptight rich guy into this peacocking playboy?

It was kind of hot and also off-putting.

"My lord!" exclaimed a voice from the entrance-way. A man in a suit with a nametag she couldn't make out on one lapel rushed forward. "We weren't expecting you tonight."

Luisa jolted for a moment before remembering their covers. Vex was here as a dissolute dragon lord from Vemion. Well, the dragon part was certainly right. She doubted they'd waste a real lord on this job, though.

He was certainly acting like every lord she'd ever met.

He smacked her ass. "Plans change. We'll need our room now."

Okay, this persona wasn't cute.

The casual disrespect made her jaw clench. She forced herself to lean into his side, playing the part of the devoted mistress even as she mentally catalogued all the ways she could make him pay for that later.

"Of course, of course," said the man. "My name is Jaekob Kaur. I'm the concierge here. If there's anything at all that you need, please ask."

Vex sneered, eyes flicking up and down, judging and dismissing the man.

The arrogance in his expression was so complete, so natural, that a chill ran down her spine.

It felt so natural she had to wonder … who really was this guy?

And as she followed him into the casino, she had no idea what she'd gotten herself into.

4

HE WAS TOUCHING HIS PARTNER.

Too much.

Vex pulled Luisa closer and tried not to notice her scent. The warm fragrance of vanilla and something a little woodsy cut through the casino's blend of expensive cologne and recycled air. The scent hit him like a caress, heat coiling low in his gut with an intensity that made his jaw clench. His dragon instincts stirred, something feral and possessive that had no place in a professional partnership.

This was … inconvenient.

Already, he felt out of sorts. Not out of control. Never that. But something about Luisa … unnerved him. She was lush curves, soft hair, and that scent that went straight to his cock.

Of course, Vex the vapid lord would have her on his arm and in his bed.

The actual Lord Vex had to remember that she was his partner, not his … woman.

And that idea went through him like a live wire.

The casino stretched before them in refined excess: marble floors veined with gold, crystal chandeliers casting delicate light across gaming tables. Everything gleamed with understated luxury that whispered its price tag. Dark wood panels inlaid with precious metals lined the walls, and the gaming tables were crafted from mahogany.

It was wealth displayed with taste, designed to make the rich feel comfortable while reminding them of their status.

A server appeared at his elbow, offering a crystal tumbler filled with smoky smelling whiskey. Vex accepted the drink and tossed it back in one smooth motion, letting the burn slide down his throat. The gesture was pure performance, a casual disregard for expensive liquor that marked someone with more money than sense.

The concierge motioned for another drink without comment.

"Oh, babe, this place is great!" Luisa leaned into

him, soft and yielding and exactly like the mistress of a dissolute lord.

He wished it didn't feel so good.

But the concierge was buying it. And they were being watched by others who would whisper. By morning, there wouldn't be a soul who hadn't heard about the dragon arriving with the woman on his back.

Good.

Making an entrance that splashy made people think he wanted to be seen. They'd watch him and pay little attention to Luisa while she broke into their systems and found the blackmailer.

Vex didn't love being the distraction, but he'd done far more disreputable things for his king than escort a beautiful woman through a paradise of wealth.

Her hand slid up his arm in a gesture that looked casual but sent fire racing along his nerve endings. The touch was almost absent-minded but felt so natural that, for a moment, he forgot they were acting. His entire focus narrowed to the warmth of her palm through his sleeve, the way her fingers traced muscle beneath expensive fabric.

Something felt fundamentally right about

having her beside him, something that made his dragon purr with satisfaction.

Dangerous thinking.

The memory of her weight on his back during their flight hit him with unexpected force. He hadn't planned to transform, hadn't intended to show off like some preening youngling trying to impress a potential partner. But the moment he'd seen her standing in that wasteland, something uncivilized had taken over.

He'd wanted to show her his strength, his grace, wanted to feel her grip tighten with excitement rather than fear. The sensation of her thighs pressed against his sides, her hands fisted in his scales, had been better than anything he'd experienced in years.

He pulled away, just a little. He couldn't get distracted by the pretty human. Vex was there to do a job. He'd help recover the data, apprehend the party responsible, and then return home and find an appropriate bride. Possibly with the help of the Royal Matchmaker.

After all, she would owe him a favor.

Though the thought of some chosen bride didn't sit well with him.

It didn't matter. Rook had managed to find a

mate. That meant it was time for Vex to consider it. He couldn't stay single forever.

The elevator to the penthouse was a work of art, its walls inlaid with gold leaf in intricate patterns that caught the soft lighting. The ride was silent except for perfectly calibrated machinery, so smooth Vex barely felt the motion. When the doors opened, they revealed a space designed with dragons in mind. The ceilings soared thirty feet high, and the main room was easily large enough for him to transform without damaging the furnishings.

Kaur gestured expansively as they entered. "The Mountain Gate has been a refuge for discerning guests for over two centuries," he said, leading them past floor-to-ceiling windows offering breathtaking views of the peaks. "Our spa facilities include mineral baths sourced from natural hot springs, and our fitness center features equipment designed for beings of all physiologies. The resort prides itself on catering to the unique needs of our distinguished clientele. And, of course, your attendant is here to see to your every need."

The attendant in question wore a simple black uniform and nearly blended in with the wall. He was … nondescript. For a moment, Vex thought he was an android, but, no, that was a human. The man was aggressively average, medium height, brown hair, unremarkable features. His face would disappear from memory the moment you looked away, and his posture suggested years of practice at being invisible.

"Does he have a name?" Vex asked haughtily.

The concierge gave him a strange look then glanced at the attendant. "I'm sure he'll answer to whatever you call him."

Lovely.

Luisa detached herself from his arm and sauntered into the room. "It's nice, baby. But didn't you say there'd be wine up here?"

The attendant silently slipped out of the main room.

"If there's anything you need, please tell me. Or your attendant. We will see to … all of your needs." Kaur smiled and backed out of the room, leaving them alone.

Luisa made a face as soon as the door closed, and Vex almost laughed.

That was when the attendant slipped back in with a glass of white wine that he silently handed over.

Luisa took it with a bright smile. "Oh, you're a

doll!" She took a sip. "Yum! You really do know how to please a girl."

"Of course, madam," the attendant said before melting back against the wall.

And not leaving them alone.

Vex could command him to leave. No doubt he would. And no doubt he'd stand just out of sight and listen to every word they said, ready to anticipate their needs … and report back anything that might be of use to the concierge.

Vex stalked up to Luisa and wrapped his arms around her.

"What are you doing?" It was hard to whisper through clenched teeth and that tight of a smile, but she managed.

He leaned in and nuzzled her neck, speaking close to her skin. "No privacy."

She nuzzled him right back. "No shit."

He pulled back and ran his hand down her side. She sucked in a breath he didn't think was an act.

"I'm going to win some money. Be ready for me when I get back."

He almost kissed her.

The desire bordering on need was there. If she really was his mistress, he'd kiss her. He'd back her up against the wall and drive himself into her until she was panting and breathless and making needy sounds he just knew she'd make when she was being properly fucked.

The thought sent sharp heat through his veins that had nothing to do with his dragon fire. His hands twitched to tilt her face up and taste those lips that had been driving him to distraction since they'd met. The space between them crackled with tension, and for a heartbeat, he thought he saw answering heat in her eyes.

But there were lines you didn't cross.

Professional. Keep it professional.

Vex backed up and left her to her work.

The elevator ride down felt longer than the trip up, giving him too much time to think about the woman he'd left behind. The way she'd fit against his side, the catch in her breath when he'd touched her, the scent of her skin that seemed to linger in his memory.

He was a dragon lord of Vemion, trained from birth in control and discipline. He did not get distracted by pretty humans, no matter how perfectly they seemed to fit in his arms.

But as he stepped onto the casino floor, Vex had the uncomfortable suspicion that this job was going to test every bit of that legendary control.

5

VEX HAD ALMOST KISSED HER.

The moment had stretched between them, charged with possibility and danger. His gaze had dropped to her mouth, lingering with an intensity that made her pulse kick against her throat. For a heartbeat, closing the space between them had felt … inevitable.

Luisa's lips tingled with what hadn't happened. Her whole body was on high alert, and if he'd kissed her, she would have kissed him back.

And she wasn't sure it would have ended with a kiss.

Heat spiraled through her chest, pooling low in her belly with an urgency that had nothing to do with their cover story. She could still feel the phantom pressure of his hands on her waist, the way his breath had ghosted across her skin when he'd leaned close.

Professional distance was supposed to be her specialty, but something about Vex made her forget every rule she'd set for herself.

Fuck.

There was something about the asshole lord act that was doing it for her. She didn't like jerks; she certainly didn't date them. But he was …

Magnetic.

Dangerous in a way that had nothing to do with being a dragon and everything to do with the debauched elegance in his movements, the controlled arrogance that suggested he could take whatever he wanted. The contradiction between the reserved professional she'd met in the bar and this strutting lord was giving her whiplash.

Which one was real? And why did both versions make her want to do things that would definitely compromise the mission?

Damn it.

She had work to do.

Luisa forced herself to breathe. The scent of Vex's expensive cologne lingered in the space he'd vacated, making it impossible to forget the solid warmth of his body against hers.

Focus. Credits. Job. Those were the only things that were allowed to matter.

Luisa unbuttoned her coat and looked at the attendant. "No one but my lord sees me naked," she said, letting her voice take on the imperious tone of someone accustomed to being obeyed. The role of a spoiled mistress came easier than she'd expected, all haughty demands and casual cruelty.

"Of course, ma'am."

"He doesn't like to be disturbed," she continued. "Only cleaning bots in the bedroom. If he catches you in there …" She shook her head. The words hung in the air, and she watched the attendant's face for any reaction. His expression remained perfectly neutral.

"Of course," the attendant repeated.

His voice was flat. She doubted this was the worst request he'd ever encountered.

The man's practiced invisibility was almost impressive. He'd perfected the art of being present but unnoticed, a living piece of furniture that antic-ipated needs without drawing attention. It was exactly the kind of skill that would make him invaluable to the Mountain's management, and exactly the kind of person who would hear every-thing and remember it all.

She wished she could dismiss him outright. But Vex hadn't done it earlier, and she suspected it was because it would just lead to subtler forms of surveillance. The Mountain catered to its guests' every need. And anticipating those needs meant watching closely.

There was a reason someone had chosen this place as a hub for blackmail.

The casino's reputation for discretion was legendary, but discretion was a double-edged sword. The same systems that protected their high-rolling clients' privacy could just as easily be turned against them. Information was currency here, more valu-able than the credits flowing across the gaming tables downstairs.

Despite their early arrival, Vex and Luisa's things were already set up in the bedroom. She shut the door firmly behind her and paused to listen for the attendant.

Silence.

At least the place had decent soundproofing.

She pulled a bug scanner out of her pack and got to work. The device was no bigger than her palm, its surface smooth and featureless except for a small display screen. She moved methodically through the room, sweeping every surface, every piece of furniture, every decorative element that might conceal surveillance equipment.

The scanner remained silent. Clean.

A good sign.

At least there was one place in the suite they might have a little privacy.

And one bed.

She stared at it.

It was a monstrosity. The thing could easily accommodate a dragon lord and a handful of mistresses, draped in silk sheets the color of midnight and piled high with pillows that probably cost more than her monthly rent. The frame was carved from some kind of expensive and shiny wood, its posts rising toward the vaulted ceiling. With a bed that size, they could sleep on opposite sides and never even know the other person was there.

Yeah, she wasn't buying it.

There was no way to ignore Vex, no matter how big the bed.

His presence filled whatever space he occupied, commanding attention even when he was trying to blend in. The memory of his body pressed against hers during their flight was still too fresh, too vivid. She could still feel the corded muscle beneath her palms, the way his warmth had seeped through her clothes.

Sharing a bed with him would be an exercise in torture, no matter how much square footage they had to work with.

But with the ever-present attendant, they couldn't sleep in different rooms. Some couples might and not think twice about it. But those couples weren't at the casino under false pretenses.

They had to play this perfectly.

The Mountain's staff would notice everything. A couple wealthy enough to afford the penthouse suite who couldn't stand to share a bed would raise questions. Questions led to scrutiny, and scrutiny was the last thing they needed when she was planning to break into the casino's most secure systems.

Luisa shoved thoughts of the bed out of her mind. That was a problem for later when Vex got back.

Only my lord sees me naked.

What had possessed her to say that? Now she was going to be thinking of it all night.

The idea of Vex seeing her naked shouldn't have sent heat racing through her veins, but there she was, imagining his hands on her skin, his eyes dark with want.

Get it together. This is a job, not a fantasy.

She pulled her equipment out of her bag and set it up at the makeup table outside the bathroom. Her main interface looked like an expensive compact mirror, its surface reflecting her face until she activated the hidden screen. The signal boosters could pass for jewelry, delicate silver pieces that would blend seamlessly with the accessories of a wealthy mistress. Her most powerful hacking tools were disguised as cosmetics, their sleek cases indistinguishable from high-end makeup.

The Mountain had too many eyes.

Cameras tracked every movement in the public spaces, and she'd bet there were sensors monitoring everything from heat signatures to electromagnetic emissions. The casino's security was legendary, layers upon layers of protection designed to keep their clients safe and their secrets secure.

Luisa started the careful process of hacking her way into that system.

The initial probes were gentle, testing the edges of the Mountain's digital defenses. The casino's firewalls were impressive, military-grade encryption wrapped around layers of redundant security protocols.

The first barrier fell after twenty minutes of careful work, giving her access to the resort's basic operational systems. Environmental controls, elevator schedules, routine maintenance logs. Nothing sensitive, but it was a foothold.

She was good at this. Better than good. The familiar rhythm of the work settled her nerves, pushing thoughts of Vex and beds and naked lords to the back of her mind where they belonged.

She was going to find this blackmailer and end this job with her dignity intact.

Even if it killed her.

6

VEX HAD ALWAYS BEEN good at cards. Tonight, he was exceptional. The high-stakes table was a battlefield disguised as entertainment. The Uldorian ambassador touched his jeweled lapel pin when he bluffed. The mining heiress drummed her fingers when she held a strong hand. Maera Daxkar, some kind of philanthropist, smiled nervously.

Vex catalogued each weakness with the same attention he'd once used in the Vemion military academy. This was warfare fought with cards instead of weapons.

And he was winning.

The chips stacked higher with each hand. He'd earned glares from the other high rollers. No one liked having their winnings stolen.

Or their women.

A seductress slid onto the chair beside him, leaning so close she was practically in his lap. "I haven't seen you around here." Blonde, expensive, and calculated. Her perfume was cloying, her smile sharp as a blade.

"I already have a woman," Vex said without looking at her.

She laughed, a sound like crystal breaking. "She's not here."

The words should have been an invitation for the dissolute lord to take what was offered. Any self-respecting rake would have accepted her proposition, especially when his mistress was safely upstairs. It would have been perfect cover, proving to anyone watching that he was exactly the kind of man who would cheat without a second thought.

But the idea of touching anyone other than Luisa made his skin crawl. The reaction was visceral and completely irrational. He'd known her less than twenty-four hours. She was his partner, nothing more. A professional colleague whose safety he was responsible for.

His dragon stirred restlessly beneath his human facade, possessive and territorial in a way that had nothing to do with logic.

"Neither are you," he said coldly, gathering his chips.

She made a sound of affront as he stood, practically shoving her away.

The blonde's mask slipped for an instant, revealing genuine surprise beneath the practiced seduction. She clearly wasn't used to rejection.

He filed the reaction away as he moved from the table, his winnings secure in his jacket.

The pit boss had been watching him for the last hour. Vex could feel those eyes crawling over him as he moved to another table.

His dossier said the man's name was Brant Tallyer, confirmed by the nametag on his chest. He had the look of a man hunting for a mark. The question was, what was he selling? Tallyer was about forty. His suit was expensive but not ostentatious, his smile warm but never reaching his eyes. Everything about him screamed middle management with ambitions, the kind of man who knew where bodies were buried and wasn't above selling maps.

Tallyer had been evaluating him all evening, watching his play style, his reactions, how he handled both winning and the blonde's advances.

Was he looking to sell something to Vex? Or scam him?

He hated the Mountain. There wasn't a single honest person to be found there.

But Vex could use that to his advantage.

Luisa had her way of finding information, he had his. If he played it right, he'd let the Mountain come to him. Places like this always had a black market. He knew it existed, knew someone was selling IDA data. The concierge had already practically offered him the services of the room attendant or anyone else on the property.

He wouldn't be shocked if the Mountain employed the blonde.

So Vex would throw around his cash and reputation, and if Luisa didn't find anything, someone would come to him.

He'd done enough for one day. Though there was one last way to flash his cash.

The elevator ride to the penthouse felt longer than usual.

He opened the suite door to find Luisa curled on the couch in silk pajamas, her dark hair loose around her shoulders. The look of her went straight to his cock.

Gone was the sharp-edged professional he'd left

behind, replaced by something softer. Silk clung to her curves in ways that made his mouth go dry, and her hair fell in dark waves.

She looked like a woman waiting for her lover to come home.

Waiting for *him*.

Possessive heat that slammed through him was immediate and overwhelming. His dragon roared to life. Every instinct demanded that he cross the room, gather her into his arms, and *take*.

Professional. Keep it professional.

She looked up with a grin. "How much did you win?"

Vex reached into his jacket and withdrew a small velvet box. He'd seen it in the casino's boutique and bought it, driven by an impulse he didn't want to examine too closely. The necklace inside was gold set with emeralds and rubies that would unquestioningly put his mark on her. It had cost more than most people made in a year. He didn't give a damn.

"For me?"

"Anything for you." Vex the rake wouldn't say that. Vex the dragon didn't care. He'd seen the necklace and could only imagine Luisa wearing it.

And nothing else.

He wouldn't ask for the latter. But he could indulge himself in this one thing.

She smiled and gestured for him to sit beside her, sweeping her hair so he could put the necklace on. Once it was in place, she slid into his lap.

Vex froze.

The weight of her settled against him like she belonged there, all soft curves perfectly fitted to his body. Her scent surrounded him. This close, he could see the pulse beating at the base of her throat, could feel the rise and fall of her breathing against his chest.

But there was something in her eyes, a subtle warning that cut through the haze of want clouding his judgment.

She wasn't being affectionate. This was part of the performance, another layer of their cover that he needed to maintain no matter how much it was killing him.

Her lips brushed his ear. "There are eyes in the room," she whispered.

He didn't look around, but if he strained, he might have been able to hear the attendant.

Of course. The ever-present surveillance that was as much a part of the Mountain as the marble floors and crystal chandeliers. They were never truly alone, never able to drop their masks completely. Every gesture, every touch was being catalogued and analyzed by someone whose loyalties lay with the casino's management.

But knowing it was an act didn't make it any easier. The body pressed against his was real; her warmth seeped through his clothes and set every nerve ending on fire.

The way she fit in his arms was real, perfect in a way he couldn't let himself think about.

His arm tightened around her waist, pulling her closer.

"What did you find?" he murmured against her neck.

This mission was going to kill him.

7

HOW FREAKING STUPID could she be?

Vex was built like a god. The solid heat of his thighs beneath hers felt far too real, and the way his arm curved around her waist sent warmth spiraling through her chest that had nothing to do with acting.

Every cell in her body was hyperaware of him, cataloging details she had no business noticing. The way his muscles shifted beneath her when he breathed. The careful control in his touch that told her he was holding himself back. She was supposed to be working, supposed to be the professional who could separate the job from everything else.

Instead, she was melting into him like some heart-struck lover.

The attendant had been coming in and out of the room for the last hour, and Luisa was now sure he was reporting to someone. The concierge? Some higher up? The who was a mystery, but that it was happening was certain. There was no reason to be so obtrusive otherwise.

She and Vex could retreat into the bedroom and get a bit of distance, but she'd started this charade, and she was damn well going to finish it.

"I'm in," she whispered against his ear, trying to ignore how his breath hitched when her lips brushed his skin.

His hand settled on her hip, fingers splaying possessively across the silk of her pajamas. "Tell me."

She might as well have been naked. The silk was thin enough that she could feel the heat of his palm through the fabric. His touch was careful and controlled, but there was hunger in the way his hand curved around her that made her stomach flutter.

"There's so much data flowing in and out it will take time to isolate it."

"You're past that much security already?" He sounded surprised.

And she knew she sounded cocky. "I'm very good."

His eyes sharpened with interest. There was a real appreciation for her skills in that look. It made her chest tight with something dangerously close to pride.

Why did his opinion matter? She knew she was good. He could play the part of the playboy lord all he wanted; she was the only one who could truly assess her skills.

But it was nice to be appreciated.

"Any sign of what we're looking for?"

She scowled but hid it by nuzzling at him. "Not yet, but if it's there, my algorithm will find it."

She shifted in his lap, ostensibly to reach for her equipment, but the movement brought her closer to his chest. The scent of expensive cologne was heady enough. But there was something smokey underneath it. Dragon fire?

Now she was pressed fully against him, her breasts brushing his chest with each breath, her thighs bracketing his hips in a way that left no doubt about the effect she was having on him. She could feel the tension in his muscles, see the careful restraint in the way he held himself perfectly still.

When their eyes met, the air between them crackled with electricity.

Oh no. This wasn't good at all.

A wisp of smoke curled around her shoulder. Luisa stilled. It was coming from Vex, barely visible but definitely there.

"What's that? Are you okay?" It was a little loud, and she hoped the attendant didn't hear. Vex's mistress would know all his little quirks.

"It's nothing."

It wasn't nothing.

"You're smoking," she whispered.

His arm tightened around her. "Occupational hazard."

He wanted her. She didn't know if that was what the smoke was, but she could read his face. No one was *that* good of an actor.

If he kissed her right now, she knew with absolute certainty that it wouldn't stop at a kiss.

She had to get this under some semblance of control before they fucked it up. "We have a bit of privacy in the bedroom and bath, no bugs. I couldn't do a thorough scan out here, so I wouldn't be so sure. We're going to have to..."

"I know." His voice was rough.

Which meant sharing a bed. The massive, ridiculous bed that suddenly seemed far too small.

"I should clean up," he said.

He lifted her gently from his lap, his hands lingering on her waist for a moment longer than necessary.

She nodded, not trusting her voice.

The loss of his warmth was immediate and jarring. She watched him disappear into the bedroom, his shoulders so tense they were twitching.

The door closed with a soft click, and moments later, she heard the whisper of running water. The thought of him stripping out of that perfectly tailored suit made her mouth go dry.

What was happening to her?

She'd worked with attractive men before without losing her mind. But Vex crashed through her defenses like they weren't there.

Luisa sank back onto the couch and pressed her palms to her heated cheeks.

This mission was going to kill her.

8

THIS WHOLE THING WAS A MESS.

Luisa's back ached from clinging to the far edge of the massive bed all night. The sheets were luxurious enough to make her feel guilty about her discomfort, but no thread count could make sharing space with Vex easier. Every time she'd started to relax, she'd become hyperaware of his presence. The rhythm of his breathing. The way the mattress dipped under his weight. The fact that he slept shirtless.

She'd discovered that detail around two in the morning when she'd risked a glance over her shoulder and found herself staring at an expanse of skin that looked far too warm and touchable. The urge to reach out and trace the line of his spine had been so strong she'd gripped the mattress edge to keep her hands to herself.

Instead of sleeping, she'd analyzed her data. The computer did most of the work, but it still took a person's eye to pull out nuances no algorithm could catch.

One name kept coming up. Well, not exactly. Data was never that easy. But one name kept getting hinted at.

Maera Daxkar. Philanthropist. Socialite. And possibly shady underground data broker to the rich and reckless.

The woman held court at Galaxie, the spa inside the Mountain. Her rooms would be difficult to access, but the spa was basically public. Remote access would only get her so far. The really sensitive data would be air-gapped, stored on devices that never touched a network. She needed to get close enough to plant physical surveillance equipment.

It was a good place to start.

And Luisa needed to get out.

If she stayed in the suite that now smelled like Vex, she might do something stupid. Like kiss him.

Or more.

She bit back a groan. This job couldn't be over soon enough.

The Mountain's spa was a temple to wealth and vanity. All white marble and brass fixtures, with soft lighting that made everyone look ten years younger.

"Welcome to Galaxie," the receptionist said. "We're here to see to your every need."

At this place, who wasn't?

Luisa felt the weight of jewels hanging from her neck. What had Vex meant by giving her the piece? The emeralds were real. The kind of gift that spoke of serious money and serious intentions. Their operating budget couldn't *possibly* afford a gift like this. What the hell was he thinking?

She didn't have time to examine his motives.

Time to play the spoiled mistress.

The receptionist guided her through opulent chambers designed to make visitors feel pampered and overwhelmed by casual displays of wealth. Luisa maintained her vacant, wide-eyed expression while cataloging security cameras and blind spots.

At the receptionist's suggestion, she took a seat in the relaxation area that overlooked Galaxie's courtyard. They were high in the mountains, but it somehow looked warm outside. That was rich people for you—they got whatever temperature they wanted, wherever they wanted it.

Luisa had just subtly stuck one of her bugs

behind a grotesque abstract sculpture when Maera Daxkar swept into the room.

Right on time.

She took her tea there every morning, followed by some rejuvenation treatment, if the booking schedule Luisa had hacked was accurate.

"Good morning!" Maera's voice was bright and welcoming, the kind that could easily extract donations with lots of zeros. "I didn't expect to see another early riser here. You are …" She gave Luisa a thorough look. "You are the dragon's woman, yes? I met him last night, quite the player."

Her information was good. No one but the concierge and room attendant had seen Luisa enter the casino beyond a passing glance. There had to be at least a hundred people staying there, so it wasn't a guess.

"Luisa," she said. She wished she'd been given a false name to go with this identity, but there was no point. Better a name she was sure to answer to.

Not that Luisa was a stranger to changing her name. It was the cost of doing business.

Or it had been. Once upon a time.

But now was not the time to dwell on the past.

"And is his lordship spoiling you like he should be?" Maera was all conspiratorial girl-talk.

Luisa laughed and stroked the necklace at her neck. "He's a dear."

"If you think *that*, you must be in love." It was a cutting remark, clearly something Maera didn't expect Luisa to understand.

Because mistresses just had to be dumb and pretty.

Luisa blinked innocently. "Of course! He buys me the most beautiful things and takes me everywhere. He even—" She bit her lip. "Oh, I shouldn't. He'd get in so much trouble."

Now Maera looked more intent. "Who's going to hear? It's just us girls."

Us girls and half a dozen data scrapers that Luisa had planted.

Luisa leaned in like she was telling a secret. "He took me to Halaea. Said he had some business to deal with there, something about ..." she waved a hand dismissively, "I don't know. But I'm not supposed to say because the king doesn't like it when his lords go there for some reason."

Halaea was a hub of slavery and worse. The Mountain catered to the vices of the rich. Halaea catered to the vices of everyone.

Maera's expression shifted, practiced warmth giving way to something sharper, more calculating.

Her fingers drummed against her teacup. "Halaea is such an interesting place. So many ... opportunities. He's a man of vision, isn't he?" Her voice dropped to a conspiratorial whisper. "I imagine Lord Vex found exactly what he was looking for there."

She was fishing, probing to see if Luisa knew more than she was letting on. The woman was definitely more than a simple philanthropist if she wasn't disgusted by the mere mention of the cesspit of a planet.

"How long have you been with Lord Vex?" Maera asked.

"Awhile," Luisa said, reaching for her water glass. "He's very ... generous."

"I'm sure he is. Though dragons can be so possessive, don't you find?"

Warning bells went off in Luisa's head. What did that have to do with anything?

"I wouldn't know," she said carefully. "I've never dated a dragon before."

Maera's laugh was like silver wind chimes. "Oh, my dear. You have no idea what you've gotten yourself into, do you?"

The words hung in the air like a threat. Maera's smile was still perfectly pleasant, but there was something lurking beneath the surface that suggested she knew far more about Luisa's situation than she should.

What exactly did this woman know about dragons? Or was she just fishing?

That was when Vex appeared in the doorway.

His expression was thunderous. All controlled fury and aristocratic arrogance as he strode into the room like he owned it.

"There you are." His voice could have cut glass.

What was he doing here? This wasn't part of the plan.

He crossed the space between them in three swift strides, his hand closing around her wrist with unmistakable possessiveness. The touch sent heat racing up her arm, but his eyes were icy.

"I told you to wait for me." His voice carried the kind of authority that expected immediate obedience, the tone of someone accustomed to being the most dangerous thing in any room.

Luisa's shock was only half-acting. She hadn't expected him to appear, hadn't anticipated the way her body would respond to his sudden presence. The careful control she'd maintained during her conversation with Maera cracked slightly under the intensity of his gaze.

"I told you to be in the suite when I needed you." The grip on her wrist was firm but not painful. He was playing his role. For some reason.

And Luisa had to play along.

"You need reminding who you belong to."

The spa staff had taken several discrete steps backward, their professional training warring with obvious fascination at the display unfolding before them. Even Maera was transfixed, her calculating gaze moving between Luisa and Vex like she was watching a sporting match.

Heat flooded her cheeks. Part embarrassment, part something else entirely. The possessive edge in his voice did things to her that had nothing to do with their cover story.

"I was just getting to know Maera," she managed, looking towards the woman with a sorry glance.

Maera's expression was bland ... or calculating.

Vex had no mercy. "You can get to know her later. We're leaving."

His hand slid from her wrist to her waist, his fingers splaying possessively across the silk of her dress. The gesture looked casual to anyone watching, but Luisa could feel the controlled strength in his touch, the way he held himself like a barely restrained predator.

As he guided her toward the exit, she caught Maera's expression in one of the mirrors. The woman was no longer bothering to hide her interest, her gaze sharp and speculative as she watched them leave. Whatever game they were playing, Luisa had the uncomfortable feeling that Maera was several moves ahead of them all.

When they reached the elevator, Luisa realized her hands were shaking.

She wasn't entirely sure why.

9

"WHAT THE EVERLOVING fuck was that about?" Luisa demanded, wrenching her arm out of his the moment they were safe behind the door to their bedroom.

It didn't feel safe at all. The massive bed dominated the space like a promise, reminding him of the night spent so close to her and yet an entire chasm of a bed apart.

The memory of it crashed over him. Hours of lying perfectly still, listening to her breathing, fighting every instinct that screamed at him to roll over and pull her into his arms.

The scent of her hair on the pillow beside his. The way she'd curled into a tight ball on the far edge of the mattress, as if she could somehow make herself small enough to disappear entirely. He'd wanted to reach for her, to smooth the tension from her shoulders and whisper reassurances until she relaxed against him.

Vex didn't cuddle.

He didn't do entanglements or emotional complications that interfered with duty. His life was structured around service to the crown, around maintaining the careful balance of power that kept Vemion stable and prosperous. He didn't get to *want*.

"Your datapad alarm went off. It seemed urgent." To his own ears, his voice sounded cold. Forbidding.

Her sneer cut right through it all. "I was on the job and—" She plucked the pad up and pursed her lips. "Did you read the warning?"

"I did."

She sighed. "Fine. You're right. It was warranted. I thought this might happen. I should have said before I left."

A partner who could admit when she was wrong. Not the worst thing ever.

Vex wouldn't gloat. He wasn't a fool.

The possessive display he'd just performed in the spa should have embarrassed him. It was only partially in character. Lord Vex of Vemion did not make public scenes over women, did not let emotion override careful political calculation. His reputation was built on control, on the kind of icy restraint that made him valuable to his uncle and dangerous to his enemies.

But there had been something deeply satisfying about staking his claim so thoroughly, about making it clear to everyone watching that Luisa belonged to him.

The way she'd looked up at him, startled and flushed, had sent heat spiraling through him. And Maera Daxkar had watched with sharp interest. That could be useful. But Vex hadn't given a damn when he saw that necklace hanging around Luisa's neck. His gift. His mark.

He had to get her out of his head. Or into his bed. That might sate the curiosity that was still growing.

No. She was already in his bed, in a fashion. Any closer and …

Well, best not to think about it.

"No one's in Maera's rooms," Luisa said. "She's in the spa, obviously, and she has treatments scheduled for the next two hours. Now's our chance to get a look at whatever files she doesn't have networked."

"What about her attendant?"

She typed something on her datapad. "He's about to get a message about a dire issue concerning Maera's laundry. It will give us an opening. You up for some breaking and entering?"

She looked eager, but he hesitated. "You should let me do this. It could be dangerous."

She bristled. Her chin lifted stubbornly, her dark eyes flashing with irritation. "I can do my job."

He didn't like this. It was sudden and felt a bit reckless.

And … fun.

This job wasn't supposed to be fun. But Vex felt a smile tugging at the side of his lips. "You're right. Let's go."

Maera's suite was two floors down from theirs. They didn't encounter anyone on the way there.

Luisa held her arm out to stop him before they turned the final corner. "Wait." She held up her datapad and pressed a button.

A minute later, a frazzled looking attendant rushed out the door and down the hall.

Vex hadn't realized the attendants were capable of that much emotion.

"I managed to hack into the laundry system and make the machines malfunction. They'll catch it quickly, and a simple reboot will fix everything. Any more and I might have gotten caught. But I'd guess we have a half hour."

They reached Maera's door, and Luisa pulled out a device as small as her palm. Her fingers moved across its surface, and within seconds, the lock disengaged with a soft click.

The room beyond was luxurious but noticeably smaller than their penthouse suite, all cream silk designed to impress without overwhelming. It fit the socially conscious socialite mask that she wore.

Crystal figurines lined the windowsill, catching the afternoon light. A sitting area dominated one corner, while the bedroom was visible through an archway draped with gossamer curtains.

"She'll keep her info somewhere." Luisa muttered it mostly to herself.

She had certainly fixated on this woman. "What makes you so certain she's our target?"

For some reason, Luisa stiffened at that.

"I'm not," she said. "But the data doesn't lie. If she's not selling IDA data, then she's selling *something*. A legitimate philanthropist wouldn't be spending her time in this den of ne'er do wells."

A good point.

Vex moved to the sitting area and began a methodical search of the delicate furnishings. Most of what he found was exactly what he'd expected from a wealthy socialite: expensive trinkets, formal correspondence, receipts from luxury vendors across the galaxy. Then, tucked into the drawer of an ornate writing desk, he discovered something more interesting. Papers detailing a charity Maera ran for orphan girls on Aetis. The documentation was thorough, professional, and painted a picture of a woman genuinely committed to helping the most vulnerable members of society.

The contradiction bothered him. Either Maera Daxkar was exactly what she appeared to be, or she was very, very good at being bad.

From across the room, Luisa let out a triumphant sound. She was peeling back a panel that looked like decorative molding, but which apparently concealed a compact computer terminal. Her hacking equipment emerged from her bag like magic, delicate tools that she connected with the precision of a surgeon.

He didn't ask her what she was doing. It was clear enough. Her brows furrowed in concentration, and she bit her lip in a way that made Vex think forbidden thoughts. She typed on her tiny keyboard and cursed under her breath until she finally let out a soft sound of triumph that went straight to his cock.

He couldn't think about her soft sounds.

She looked up at him with a smile. "Come on," she said as she unplugged one last cord. "We need to get out of here."

They slipped from the room as quietly as they'd entered, Luisa's equipment concealed again.

In the hallway, Vex's hearing caught the soft whisper of footsteps approaching from around the corner.

He didn't let himself think or hesitate.

Vex backed Luisa against the wall and covered her mouth with his. She tasted like mint and sugar, sweet and intoxicating in a way that obliterated every rational thought. Her lips were soft beneath his, yielding in a way that sent fire racing through his veins.

It was supposed to be tactical necessity, but it became something far more dangerous the moment their mouths met.

She melted against him like she'd been waiting for this, her body fitting perfectly against his chest. Her hands came up to rest on his shoulders, fingers curling into the expensive fabric of his jacket as if she needed the anchor.

Without conscious thought, he hiked her leg up against his hip, pressing her more firmly against the wall. His cock was hard and insistent, straining against the confines of his perfectly tailored pants. He wanted to take her right there in the hallway, to slide his hands under that silk dress and discover if she was as warm and wet as he imagined.

This was madness. It was everything he shouldn't want and couldn't resist, a claiming that felt as natural as breathing.

He pulled back and could smell the smoke coming off of his skin. This woman made him lose control in ways he hadn't known were possible.

Whoever had been walking down the hallway was long gone.

Luisa was looking at him wide eyed. "That's one way to maintain our cover."

He didn't respond.

He was too busy telling himself he couldn't kiss her again.

10

LUISA HADN'T FOUND anything specifically incriminating in Maera Daxkar's documents. The woman was definitely moving money through shell companies. But smuggling luxury goods and skimming charity donations wasn't the same as trafficking stolen dating profiles across the galaxy.

Something was off about the woman.

But thinking about Daxkar was better than thinking of Vex. Of the kiss.

The memory slammed into her every time she let her guard down. The way he'd pressed her against the wall, his body a solid wall of heat and power. His mouth had been demanding, claiming.

For those few seconds, she'd forgotten about the mission, forgotten about professional distance, forgotten everything except the need to get closer to him.

But it was more than just the physical intensity that had her rattled. It was the way she'd responded to him, completely and without reservation. She'd never been the type to lose herself in a kiss, yet the moment his lips had touched hers, every defense she'd built had crumbled. The taste of him still lingered in her memory, smoke and sex and something that made her mouth water.

What scared her most was how right it had felt. How perfectly she'd fit against him, how natural it had been to wrap herself around his strength.

For a heartbeat, standing there in that hallway with his hands on her body, she'd felt like she belonged somewhere.

Dangerous thinking.

She hated him, she thought. She had to. Because if she didn't ...

No, better to hold onto hate and hope it didn't become something unmanageable.

It was easy to hate him when Vex was nowhere to be found. They'd spent another sleepless night in the giant bed, not saying a word about the kiss.

She'd lain there in the darkness, hyperaware of every small movement he made. The space between them had felt charged with possibility. With desire. More than once, she'd found herself turning toward his warmth before she jerked herself back to sanity.

He'd been awake too. She could tell from the careful way he held himself, the rhythm of his breathing that was just a little too controlled to be natural. It only made everything worse.

They'd both been lying there, wanting. And reaching for more would ruin everything.

And now his lordship had sent a note, summoning her like she belonged to him.

Which, she sort of did. Given their cover. But still, it was the principle of the thing. If he wanted her on the floor with him, he could ask.

But she wasn't going to put the mission at risk for a temper tantrum.

If Vex wanted arm candy, she was going to kill him with sweetness.

A half hour later, she slunk through the casino like she was built for it. The whisper of silk against her skin was a reminder of the role she was playing, each sway of her hips calculated to draw attention and hold it. Eyes snaked over her. Conversations stuttered.

And when Vex spotted her, his mouth actually dropped open. Only a bit, barely more than if he were taking a breath. But that reaction was all for her. She even saw a wisp of smoke come off his hand before quickly dispelling.

She wasn't the only one affected by the inconvenient thing between them.

The dress was a masterpiece of strategic seduction, emerald silk that clung to her body. It hugged her curves from breast to hip before flaring into a skirt that was just long enough to be decent and short enough to promise scandal with every step. The neckline plunged deep enough to showcase the necklace Vex had given her, the gems laying against her skin like a brand of ownership.

Every eye in the casino tracked her movement, but she only cared about one pair. Vex's gaze sizzled in a way that made heat pool low in her belly. The careful mask of aristocratic boredom had slipped completely, replaced by something *hungry*.

His attention fixed on the necklace at her throat, and a wisp of smoke curled off of him. The gems lay against her pulse point like a collar, a visible statement of possession that everyone in the room could read. The weight of it was warm against her skin.

She was wearing his claim for all to see.

She sauntered over to Vex and draped herself

over him, letting her body go limp in all the right places as she wrapped her arms around his neck. She nuzzled against him. "Hey, baby, are you winning?"

He grunted and pulled her close. His arm banded around her waist with unmistakable greediness, hauling her against his side until there was no space between them. The heat of his body seeped through the thin silk, making her skin tingle with awareness. She was practically sitting in his lap.

And now that she was where she belonged, no one was staring at them. This kind of behavior was normal, expected even, from assholes like Vex.

After a moment, Luisa spotted Maera carefully weaving her way towards them past crowded tables. The woman moved like a shark through the crowd, pausing to exchange pleasantries while her gaze kept drifting back to their corner.

And then her past chose that moment to punch her right in the gut.

Maera passed in front of a tall, broad man wearing a casino uniform. At first, he didn't look like anyone in particular, then Luisa's brain, and her survival instincts, caught up.

Brant Tallyer.

Her veins chilled to ice, every muscle in her

body going rigid with shock. The years fell away in an instant, leaving her feeling like the desperate data-rat she'd once been.

Tallyer looked older, his face harder, but those cold eyes were exactly the same. Eyes that had watched while his enforcers worked people over for information. And worse.

She didn't realize that she'd stiffened until Vex placed a hand on her arm and shot her a questioning look.

Right. Play the part. Be the mistress.

She let out a vapid little laugh and nuzzled closer. Then she reached for Vex's whiskey and knocked it back like it was her own. The liquor burned down her throat, and it was a welcome distraction from the fear racing through her system.

She wanted another. Or three.

What the fuck was that bastard doing here?

Tallyer had been declared dead in a gang war three years ago. She'd made sure it was true, had paid good money for confirmation from sources who didn't make mistakes about that kind of thing. Seeing him here, alive and apparently employed by the Mountain, meant either her sources had been wrong or he had very powerful friends.

Tallyer used to run the roughest crew in the

lower city. And to say she was on his bad side was a bit of an understatement.

Aetis ate people alive. You had to do what you had to do to survive.

And Luisa had certainly survived.

She'd crossed lines she'd sworn she'd never cross. But when the choice was between eating and starving, between having a roof over her head and sleeping in the toxic rain of the undercity, the moral calculations became very simple. Tallyer's crew had controlled the best data streams, the richest targets, the safest territories. Working for him had meant protection and steady credits.

Until it hadn't.

Until she'd gotten too good, too independent, and made the mistake of cutting him out of a score that should have set her up for life. The beating that followed had put her in a medical center for two weeks and left scars she still carried.

Had Tallyer seen her?

She needed to tell Vex.

The thought formed automatically, the instinct of a partner who trusted her backup. But the moment it crystallized, everything within her recoiled.

What was she supposed to say? *Hey, partner, you*

know how you need to implicitly trust me to recover this highly valuable data for our employer? Yeah, well, I used to be really good at stealing it.

No.

The confession would end everything. Vex would look at her with those cold dragon eyes and see exactly what she really was: a thief playing at being legitimate.

She chanced another look around the room, but Tallyer was gone.

He'd vanished as completely as if he'd never been there, melting back into the crowd with the skill that had kept him alive in the undercity for so many years.

Maybe he hadn't seen her. She didn't look at all like the data-rat she used to be. A few enhancements here, a different haircut there, and no way in all the hells would the old Luisa have been caught on some rich man's arm in this dress.

If the old Luisa had gotten anywhere close to the jewels around her neck, she would have snatched them and run as far as she could.

"You let her out of bed," Maera said as she finally approached the table.

Luisa jerked back to the present, forcing her expression into the insipid smile that was becoming second nature. She tittered. "You're so bad!"

Vex gave her a look that was so cold it burned. "She knows her place."

She clutched his arm and leaned closer. "Right by you, baby."

A mix of cheers and groans went up as the dealer turned over the final card and pushed a large stack of chips towards Vex.

Another win for Vex.

So why did it feel like she'd just staked all her chips on a losing hand?

11

THE CHARADE WAS FALLING APART.

Vex watched Luisa fidget with her drink across the low table, the space between them feeling like a chasm. They were supposed to be inseparable lovers, but right now they looked like strangers forced to share a drink. She kept glancing around the room instead of gazing adoringly at him, and he'd caught himself checking his communicator twice in the last five minutes.

This game was supposed to be his specialty.

Instead, every time he looked at her, all he could think about was the way she'd melted against him in that hallway. The memory of her taste, the soft sound she'd made when he'd pressed her against the wall, the way her body had fit perfectly against his.

His dragon stirred restlessly beneath his human facade, a low burn of want that made it impossible to think clearly. The control that had defined his entire life was cracking, piece by piece, every time she looked at him.

The beast wanted to take her so thoroughly that no other male would dare look in her direction. Sitting there pretending to be indifferent while his entire body ached with the need to touch her was torture.

"You're sitting too far away," he said quietly.

Luisa's gaze snapped to his. "What?"

"We're supposed to be lovers. You're sitting like I have a communicable disease."

Heat flashed in her dark eyes. "Maybe I'm just giving you space to breathe."

Before he could respond, Maera's voice cut through the tension.

"So this is where you escaped to. There's more than one man back there eager for his money back. If you can pull yourself away." She gave a pointed look to the space between them.

Maera was standing beside another woman. The stranger was tall, elegant, with platinum hair swept into an elaborate style and harsh blue eyes. Everything about her screamed nobility. She carried herself with the particular arrogance that came from generations of inherited power, the kind that looked at everyone else as either useful or disposable.

Though it might have been a *bit* hypocritical of Vex to judge someone for being an aristocrat.

"Lord Vex," Maera said, "I'd like you to meet Lady Eleyna Sordin. Eleyna, this is the dragon lord I was telling you about."

Lady Eleyna's smile was sharp as a blade. "A pleasure." She slid onto the couch beside him without invitation, close enough that her perfume, expensive and cloying, filled his nostrils. "I've heard so much about dragons. Such … impressive creatures."

The way she said it made his skin crawl.

Luisa's posture went rigid. Her shoulders squared, her chin lifted, and something dangerous flickered in her eyes.

"Eleyna has such fascinating stories about court life on Volia," Maera continued, settling beside Luisa. "She knows everyone who's anyone across the galaxy."

"How wonderful," Luisa said sweetly. Too sweetly.

Lady Eleyna leaned closer to Vex, her hand

coming to rest on his arm. "I watched you play out there. You're so … commanding. I do admire a man who knows how to take risks."

He didn't want this woman touching him. The asshole lord he was playing would love to have multiple women draped over him, even in front of his mistress. But the real Vex was too close to the surface.

Luisa was the only woman he wanted touching him.

That's when she moved.

Luisa rose from her seat with fluid grace and crossed to where Vex sat, settling herself directly in his lap with possessive certainty. Her arm slid around his neck, fingers playing with the hair at his nape in a gesture that was pure territorial claim.

"Baby," she said, her voice carrying just enough edge to make it clear she wasn't asking, "remember what you promised me." She nuzzled against his neck, her breath hot and claiming.

The contact sent fire racing through his veins, her weight settling against him in a way that felt devastatingly right. The scent of her skin filled his senses and made his head spin.

His body responded instantly, heat pooling low in his gut as his cock hardened beneath her. She was pressed so close against him that there was no way she could miss his reaction, no way to hide how desperately he wanted her.

Lady Eleyna's hand fell away from his arm as if burned.

The display should have been pure performance, but the fierce satisfaction that roared through him was entirely real. His dragon rumbled with approval.

Mine, the beast whispered, and for once, Vex didn't argue with the certainty.

Luisa's jealousy was a revelation. The way she staked her claim, fearless and territorial, made him want to carry her out of there and show her exactly what belonging to a dragon really meant.

Lady Eleyna's expression had shifted from interest to cold calculation, her blue eyes narrow with annoyance. She clearly wasn't used to being dismissed so thoroughly, especially not by someone she probably considered a nonentity. But Luisa had made her position crystal clear, and even the most entitled noble recognized a battle they couldn't win.

"How ... quaint," Eleyna said, her voice dripping with disdain. But she shifted away from him, finally giving him the space his dragon demanded.

As if two unwanted companions weren't

enough, the pit boss, Brant Tallyer, came up beside Maera.

"Ladies, Lord Vex." His smile was practiced, professional. "Ms. Daxkar, your private game is ready when you are."

His eyes lingered on Luisa in a way that made something cold and dangerous unfurl in Vex's chest.

The man's gaze was too intense, too searching, as if he was trying to place her face in his memory. Beneath him, Luisa went rigid, her fingers tightening in his hair as if she was fighting the urge to hide her face against his shoulder.

"Wonderful," Maera said, rising. "Luisa, darling, you simply must join us. It's ladies only tonight, I'm afraid, Lord Vex. Allow me to steal your … woman." She left just enough pause before the last word to make it sound unseemly.

"There is plenty of room for Luisa," Brant agreed with a strange note in his voice.

Luisa's entire body went even more rigid, every muscle coiled with tension.

Vex's hand settled on Luisa's thigh, fingers splaying possessively across the silk of her dress. "No."

It came out rougher than intended, carrying an

edge of command that had nothing to do with their cover story.

"I have uses for her that don't involve cards."

Luisa's breath hitched against his neck.

Lady Eleyna's laugh was like breaking crystal. "How delightfully savage. You were exactly right about him, Mae."

Smoke curled from Vex's nostrils before he could stop it.

The tension ratcheted up. Maera and Eleyna exchanged a look, while Tallyer continued to watch Luisa with that unsettling intensity. Vex's dragon was barely leashed now, the part of him that wanted to unleash his fire and burn away anything that threatened the woman in his arms.

The civilized veneer he'd maintained his entire life felt paper-thin, ready to shatter at the slightest provocation.

"Perhaps another time," Maera said smoothly. Her gaze remained as calculating as ever.

If anyone was going to see through them, it was her.

As the women departed, Tallyer lingered for a moment longer, his attention still fixed on Luisa with an intensity that made Vex want to bare his teeth.

"Enjoy your evening," the pit boss said finally and walked off.

Vex didn't like the final look the man gave. It was too much like a hunter sizing up his prey.

And Vex was the only hunter that Luisa needed.

The moment they were alone, Vex stood, lifting Luisa with him. "We're leaving."

In the elevator back to their suite, Luisa remained pressed against his side, her scent filling his senses and making his control fray. Every time the elevator stopped at another floor, he found himself pulling her closer, as if someone might try to take her away.

When the door to their suite opened, Vex growled.

The attendant was puttering around the main room with comfortable casualness. He wasn't even pretending to be discreet anymore.

Vex's temper, already frayed from the encounter downstairs, finally snapped.

Even in his penthouse, he was playing a role. The winner claiming his prize. The dragon lord who took what he wanted.

But it didn't feel like acting.

The line between performance and reality had blurred beyond recognition.

His hands found her waist, pulling her flush against him as his mouth crashed down on hers. The kiss was claiming, possessive, designed to leave no doubt in anyone's mind about who she belonged to.

But beneath the calculated display, something far more honest was burning. His cock was hard and insistent against her hip, his body responding to her nearness with an intensity that had nothing to do with their cover story. The attendant was forgotten, the mission was forgotten, everything was forgotten except the woman in his arms and the desperate need to make her his in every way that mattered.

She responded with equal intensity, her fingers fisting in his jacket as she pressed herself against him. The soft sound she made, part moan and part surrender, sent fire racing through his veins.

He could taste her desire, could feel the way her body melted into his as if she'd been made for his touch.

This was madness, but he couldn't bring himself to care.

Luisa looked up at him, something challenging in her dark eyes. "Is this the part where you remind me who I belong to? When I just had to watch that woman put her hands on you."

The words hit him like a punch. Yes. That's exactly what this was.

He backed her against the wall, his hands framing her face. "You're mine," he said, loud enough for the attendant to hear. "Don't forget it."

She rose on her toes, bringing her mouth close to his ear. "Then prove it."

He kissed her like he was drowning and she was air.

Her response was immediate and overwhelming. She wrapped her legs around his waist, clinging to him with desperate intensity. The silk of her dress rode up, and he could feel the heat of her through the thin fabric.

He could taste the wine she'd been drinking, could feel the rapid flutter of her pulse where his thumb pressed against her throat. The sound of her breathing, quick and shallow and needy, filled his ears and made his cock throb.

Her legs around his waist brought her core directly against his hardness, the thin barrier of her dress and his pants doing nothing to hide how desperately he wanted her. She was warm and soft in all the right places, her body molding to his like she'd been designed specifically for his touch. The scent of her arousal mingled with her perfume, creating an intoxicating blend that made his dragon roar with satisfaction.

Every nerve ending in his body was on fire, hypersensitive to every point of contact between them.

The weight of her breasts against his chest, the way her fingers tangled in his hair, the soft sounds she was making against his mouth. He wanted to strip away the silk barriers between them, to feel her skin against his, to claim her so thoroughly that she'd never doubt who she belonged to.

"I need you," she whispered against his mouth, her voice raw with want. "Please."

The plea sounded so real, so genuine, that for a moment he forgot they were performing. This was Luisa, his partner, his—just his.

Mine.

The thought was absolute, terrifying, and completely unprofessional.

He tore away from the kiss, his entire body on fire with need. Smoke was rising from his skin now, visible wisps that betrayed just how close to losing control he really was.

"Leave us," he commanded the attendant, his voice rough with barely restrained power.

He carried Luisa into the bedroom, kicking the door shut behind them with more force than necessary.

The moment they were alone, he set her down and backed away, putting distance between them before he did something they'd both regret.

She looked thoroughly claimed, her dark hair mussed from his fingers, her lips swollen from his kisses. The emerald dress was wrinkled from their embrace, the necklace he'd given her glinting against her flushed skin like a brand of ownership.

She looked like she belonged to him, like she was his in every way that mattered, and the sight sent a fresh wave of fire through his chest. He wanted to close the distance between them again, to finish what they'd started, to make the claiming real instead of just performance.

But he couldn't have it.

Professional boundaries existed for a reason. And he needed to get control of this situation. Things were already out of hand.

"The pit boss," he said, his voice more controlled than he felt. "You reacted to him. What was that about?"

Luisa blinked, the question clearly catching her off guard. "What?"

"Tallyer. You stiffened when he approached."

She was quiet for a long moment, something shifting in her expression. Then she lifted her chin, that stubborn fire he was learning to recognize blazing in her eyes.

"I don't give a single fuck about the pit boss."

She closed the distance between them in two quick steps and kissed him again.

This time, he didn't pull away.

12

IT WAS SUPPOSED to be a distraction.

Luisa crushed her lips against Vex's, fist clenched so hard against his shirt that it almost hurt. The expensive fabric bunched between her knuckles, silk threads catching on her fingernails as panic and desperation drove her forward. She just needed to stop his questions about Tallyer, needed to redirect his attention anywhere else.

But then his hands seized her waist with startling power, and every ridge of his knuckles pressed through the silk of her dress as he hauled her against his body. His mouth consumed hers, tongue plunging deep with a groan that she felt all the way to her core.

Her knees gave out. He held her upright like it was nothing.

The kiss spiraled beyond her control. What was meant to be distraction became hungry and desperate, her body responding with an intensity that made her head spin. His taste flooded her senses.

She'd kissed men before, but it had never felt like she might die if they stopped.

He spun her around, and the wall was cold against her spine. His forearm caged her beside her temple, muscles rigid as granite.

His other hand tilted her chin up, rough thumb grinding over her swollen lower lip. Hot breath ghosted across her ear.

"You're playing with my fire."

His voice liquefied the resistance in her thighs, and she hooked her legs around his hip to keep herself upright.

Oh fuck. Mistake. Now she was more open to him than ever.

Grazing teeth along her jaw, he made his way to her neck, licking where her pulse thumped frantically. When his fingers found her zipper between her shoulder blades, a sharp tear rent the air. Cool air licked across her exposed back, her hips, finally her breasts.

Her nipples puckered, painfully tight.

Heat flooded through her veins. The silk fell all around her, and she perched on him in nothing but the emerald necklace he'd given her and a scrap of lace.

Vex's gaze raked over her like a dragon looking at his treasure. His large hand lifted one breast, calluses scraping across her delicate skin before he took the peak into his mouth. Sucking hard, tongue swirling. The suction pulled fire from her ribs straight to her belly.

She was drowning in sensation.

Then he was on his knees, fingers hooking into her underwear and dragging them down her thighs. Cool air pricked at her damp heat. He flicked his eyes up to her as his thumbs parted her slick folds.

It felt almost powerful to have him on his knees before her.

"Look at you," he growled, voice thick like velvet over gravel.

Powerful? Not a bit. He was the one who'd taken control here.

The way he looked at her made her forget how to breathe. Like she was something precious and filthy at the same time, something to be worshipped and devoured. She throbbed with an ache that wouldn't let up, empty and desperate for his touch.

His broad tongue stroked straight up her slit, collecting her wetness. Her sharp gasp echoed in the room.

Then firm strokes circling her swollen center. Each pass made her nerve endings sizzle. She ground involuntarily against his tongue, any pretense of control completely gone.

She buried her fingers in his thick hair, holding him against her as he worked her with his mouth. His tongue was clever and single-minded, finding every spot that made her moan. The sounds she was making should have embarrassed her, but she was beyond caring. Soft cries and breathless pleas fell from her lips as he built the pressure inside her higher.

Suddenly, he sealed his lips around her. The ache intensified, coiling deep in her core. Two thick fingers slid inside her easily, curling upward and scraping against that spot that made her see stars.

When he sped up the circles of his tongue while finger-fucking her hard and deep, she came blinding fast. Her whole body twisted, and she could hear herself screaming as she spasmed around his knuckles.

The climax stole her breath and sanity. Every muscle in her body went rigid as pleasure crashed through her. She'd come before, but never like this. Never with the feeling that she might actually shatter into pieces and never find them all again.

Vex surged up, lifting her thighs around his hips. Her back hit the wall once more, sweat sticking their torsos together. The blunt crown of his cock rubbed against her soaked entrance, hot and insistent.

"Tell me you want this," he demanded.

At her choked "Please," he slammed deep in one confident stroke. The stretch bloomed into sparking fullness that shook a sob from her core. His eyes locked with hers the entire time, fiery yellow holding her captive.

The feeling of him filling her completely stole what little breath she had left. He was big, bigger than she expected, and the stretch burned in the most delicious way. But it was more than physical sensation. It was the way he watched her face as he entered her, like he was memorizing every expression, every little sound.

It was intimate in a way that terrified her, like he was seeing straight through to her soul.

Slow, grinding withdrawal, inch by agonizing inch, then snapping his hips forward to seat himself impossibly deep. He ground against her hypersensitive center every time he fully sheathed inside her.

It built pleasure faster than she'd imagined possible.

Each thrust sent shockwaves through her still-quivering body, and she clung to his shoulders like he was the only solid thing in a world gone wobbly. The rhythm he set was demanding, calculated to drive her out of her mind. Deep and slow, then fast and hard, keeping her constantly off-balance.

Then he was holding her hips steady to thrust into her with hard, deep strokes. Shockwaves with every collision against the wall. Her body jolted with each impact, and her core ached with the force yet clenched greedily on each withdrawal.

Her nails dug grooves down his sweat-slicked back as his thrusts became jagged and unhinged. He was snarling incoherently against her collarbone while pistoning harder, deeper.

When her climax tore through her again, gut-deep convulsions dragging sharp cries from her throat, he crushed her mouth, swallowing her sounds as his own release hit. Blinding hot seed burst inside her in thick spurts, his groan dragged out and raw against her shoulder.

The intensity of coming together felt like being struck by lightning. Every nerve ending in her body fired at once. This wasn't just physical release, it was something deeper. Like two forces of nature colliding and creating something entirely new.

Their bodies trembled violently together in the aftermath, her legs slumping off his hips. His forehead pressed to hers, breath erratic.

He carried her then, collapsing sideways onto the massive bed. He tucked her back against his chest, cocooning her with his larger frame.

His lips traced the curve of her shoulder blade, soft kisses that felt reverent after the intensity of what had just passed between them.

The tangled bliss lasted maybe twenty seconds.

Then reality crashed over her like cold water, washing away the haze of satisfaction and leaving only stark, terrifying clarity.

She'd just had the best sex of her life with her partner. Her temporary partner, who would disappear back to his dragon life the moment this job was over.

Worse, she'd used sex to manipulate him, to

distract him from questions she couldn't answer, and it had backfired spectacularly. Instead of staying in control, she'd lost herself completely.

What the hell had she just done?

13

LUISA WOKE before dawn tangled in silk sheets and Vex's arms.

His breathing was soft and steady against her neck, one heavy arm draped across her waist like he was afraid she might disappear. The big bad dragon snored. Quietly, but still.

She shouldn't find it adorable.

The darkness wrapped around them, and Luisa lay perfectly still. His chest pressed against her back, warm and solid, while his fingers splayed possessively across her ribs.

This felt dangerous in a way that had nothing to do with their mission. Waking up in his arms felt like she belonged there. The thought sent panic skittering through her chest. This was *not* supposed to happen. Every breath he took stirred the hair at her nape, and she had to fight the urge to press back against him.

Carefully, she extracted herself from his grip, holding her breath as he shifted but didn't wake. The cool air hit her bare skin, raising goosebumps.

The bathroom was its own kind of sanctuary. She turned the shower as hot as she could stand and tried to wash away the memory of his hands on her skin.

It didn't work.

She wasn't sure she wanted it to.

She could still feel where his mouth had been, still taste him on her lips. Her body ached in intimate places. This was supposed to have been a distraction, a tactical maneuver to keep him from asking questions about Tallyer.

Simple manipulation. But nothing about last night had been simple.

The way he'd looked at her when he'd pressed her against the wall, like she was something precious and wild that he needed to possess. The way her name had sounded on his lips when he'd buried himself inside her. She'd had sex before, sure, but this felt different.

This felt like he'd marked her in some fundamental way.

She could work with someone without getting her *feelings* involved. She'd built her entire career on the ability to separate emotion from necessity. But standing under the spray of hot water, she couldn't deny that something had shifted between them.

She dreaded to find out just how bad it would be.

When she emerged, Vex was awake, sitting on the edge of the bed in nothing but sleep pants. His hair was mussed, and when their eyes met, the air between them crackled with everything they'd left tangled in those sheets.

"Morning," he said, his voice rough with sleep.

"Good morning." Her voice sounded steadier than she felt.

They moved around each other with careful politeness, like strangers sharing space instead of partners who had torn each other apart with pleasure hours before.

She thought she might suffocate.

Every casual movement felt designed to avoid accidental contact that might shatter their fragile balance. When she reached for her clothes, he turned away politely. When he moved to the dresser, she found urgent business on the other side of the room. But she was far too aware of every shift of muscle beneath his skin, every casual stretch that reminded her exactly how that body had felt pressed against hers.

This sucked.

She wanted to pull him back into bed and say fuck it. But that wasn't an option. If they fell back into bed together, they might never get out. And they were here to do a job.

Luisa pulled out her equipment and began reviewing her notes. The familiar rhythm of data analysis helped center her, gave her something to focus on besides the way Vex's muscles moved as he reached for his shirt.

"Anything new?" he asked, settling beside her at the small table.

Too close. She could smell his skin, warm and soft from sleep.

"Shell company after shell company," she said, proud of how professional she sounded. "She's hiding something. And taking payments from exactly the kind of people who might want what was stolen. It's not proof, but ..."

He leaned closer to look at her screen, and her pulse jumped.

His gaze moved over the data with the same intensity he'd focused on her body the night before. She could feel the heat radiating from his skin, see his throat flexing. The memory of pressing her lips to that exact spot made her mouth go dry. When he reached across her to point at something on the screen, his arm brushed hers, and electricity shot through her.

A soft chime announced an incoming message. Vex activated the suite's communication system, and Maera's voice filled the room.

"Lord Vex, I hope you and your lovely companion slept well. I would be honored if you would join me for a private meeting this afternoon. There are certain matters of mutual interest I believe we should discuss."

The message ended with coordinates to Maera's private quarters.

"I'm going." Luisa said it at the exact moment Vex said, "you're going."

She opened her mouth, ready for an argument, and Vex looked at her with one eyebrow raised. They stared at each other for a beat.

"I didn't think you'd want that," she finally said.

"Maera seems fixated on you. She wanted you at the table last night. She's mentioned you in the message. She talked to you in the spa. We can use that. Or did you think I'd try and bench you because of …" He trailed off, and his eyes flicked to the bed.

Nope. They weren't talking about it.

"Then I guess we'd better get ready. I already showered."

His eyes flicked her up and down, a flash of heat in them so intense it nearly curled her toes. "I can see that. Next time you should wait for me." He didn't give her a chance to reply, instead walking towards the shower without a backward look.

Luisa groaned and clutched her head in her hands. This man might kill her.

She forced herself to focus on organizing her equipment, shoving data chips and surveillance devices into their proper compartments with more force than necessary.

It felt safer to sit in the living room. She didn't see the attendant, but she was sure he was around somewhere, especially since there was a steaming cup of the tea she liked sitting on the table opposite the couch.

Constant surveillance had a few perks.

She curled in on herself and pushed away any thoughts of the night before, even as her body luxuriated in the ache and stretch of seldom used muscles. She was just starting to convince herself that things might work themselves out when she spotted the white rectangle sitting on the floor by the door. It was so out of place that, for a moment, she didn't realize it was a card.

She crossed the room and picked it up. The words were blocky, the handwriting impossible to identify. But the words made it very clear.

"Lu—Long time no see. Meet me in the Frost Lounge at 4 PM. We have so much to catch up on."

The card felt like ice in her fingers. Her vision tunneled as panic crashed over her. The facade she'd built, the reputation, the safe distance from her past, all of it crumbled in an instant. She was back in the undercity, bloody and broken, listening to Tallyer's promises about what would happen if she ever crossed him again.

Her hands shook so violently she could barely hold the card. Every muscle in her body went tight with remembered fear. She'd been so careful, so thorough in covering her tracks. She'd paid good money for confirmation that Tallyer was dead, had built her new life on that certainty.

But there was no mistaking the handwriting. The same hand that had written her death sentence three years ago was reaching out from beyond the grave.

How long had Tallyer been watching her? How much did he know about her new life, her work with the IDA, her partnership with Vex?

Everything she'd built, every careful step toward legitimacy, could be destroyed with a few well-placed words. Vex would look at her with those cold eyes and see exactly what she really was: a lie trying to pass herself off as something real.

She stared at the card until the letters blurred.

Meeting Brant would be beyond stupid. It would be suicidal.

But she was afraid she didn't have any other choice.

The man could destroy her with a word. They hadn't left on good terms, and Tallyer was a mean son of a bitch. He'd want to make her pay for every imagined score.

The water shut off in the bathroom.

Luisa quickly hid the card in her equipment bag, her hands still shaking.

She could make a few guesses as to what Tallyer might want.

At 4 PM, she was going to find out.

14

LUISA'S LAUGH was too tittering as she responded to Maera's nonsense about her dress. The dress was fine, functional. Vex ignored how it hugged Luisa's curves and reminded him of her pressed against his skin.

The last thing he needed was to remember that.

But his body had other ideas. The memory of her naked beneath him was just *there*, how she'd felt wrapped around him, slick and tight and perfect. The sound she'd made when he'd buried himself inside her, that breathless cry that nearly drove him to his knees.

His cock stirred, and he shifted to hide his reaction. Something had settled in his chest when he'd claimed her. Like he'd found the missing piece he hadn't known he was looking for. The dragon in him rumbled with satisfaction. *Mine.* The word echoed with absolute certainty, and he fought the urge to reach for her, to remind everyone exactly who she belonged to.

He forced his thoughts away.

They were on the job.

And Maera Daxkar was a snake.

"You can't just let us girls chitchat, Lord Vex." Maera smiled, pulling him into the conversation. Her expression was carefully crafted warmth and feminine conspiracy, but her eyes remained calculating. "Tell us about your holdings back on Vemion. I'm sure Luisa would love to know." Maera gave her a conspiratorial wink.

It took a beat for Luisa to respond with her empty laugh.

Something was off with her, and it wasn't the sex.

The morning had been awkward, but Luisa had been all work, going over her data like she'd been born to read it. Only after he'd gotten out of the shower were things off.

Why?

There hadn't been time to ask.

"What do you want to know about the old

heap?" He summoned his most dissolute voice—the angry, greedy lord who wanted more and would do whatever it took to get it. "I'm a second son. I've been forced to make my own fortunes."

"And he's made so much." Luisa didn't miss her cue this time.

Her fingers traced the necklace at her throat. His only regret about last night was that she hadn't been wearing it when he took her.

"Oh, is that—"

A knock interrupted, and an Oscavian with dark purple skin and pink hair stuck his head in.

"What is it, Zymon?" Maera sounded unhappy about the interruption.

"I'm sorry, ma'am. I thought you wanted an update on the ..." The Oscavian's gaze swept over Vex and Luisa with professional assessment, cataloging their faces.

"Later." The harshest he'd ever heard her. With him, she'd been cloying sweetness and soft edges.

Zymon disappeared.

"You'll have to forgive my head of security. He's eager."

Head of security. Vex would bet his title that the interruption hadn't been accidental. She wanted her man to see them in person. Sometimes a security scan didn't do faces justice.

"Now, tell me about this heap. I've never been to Vemion, but I've heard stories."

"Oh, yes, please." Luisa clung to his arm. "You never let me visit."

He leaned back, adopting the bored posture of a man discussing property he took for granted. "It's nothing impressive, a bit of hunting land and a house with good bones. Old Vemion style, stone and timber, built for winter storms. There's a tower where I can shift and take flight without neighbors complaining. The city quarters are convenient for court business but cramped. Three rooms overlooking the financial district, so I can walk to the banks when I need to move credits." All true. No reason to lie about mundane details when truth served just as well.

"Don't feel bad, dearie," Maera told Luisa. "He can't bring his mistress around the house his wife will oversee."

Luisa stiffened. Her expression drooped and, for a second, looked real. Pain flickered across her features, before she caught herself. Then she recovered. "Vexy says he can't live without me."

Vexy.

He wasn't sure whether to strangle her for the nickname or burst out laughing.

He settled on an indulgent eye roll.

"My uncle will make an issue of it someday. He favors some royal matchmaking charlatan. She matches nobles according to hoard size and whether the king favors them."

He watched Daxkar closely. Her eyes lit up.

Jackpot.

"You're looking for an alternative way of matching."

He stroked his fingers down Luisa's neck and gave her a look he feared was too affectionate. He couldn't afford to feel anything for her. Not here. Not ever.

And yet.

"I won't be allowed to take who I want as a bride," he lied, staring at Luisa.

Her eyes softened. She gave him something almost like a real smile.

"But if there was some way to prevent my uncle's meddling …"

"I meet the most interesting people in my work," Maera said. "Perhaps one could help." She didn't add more.

The conversation drifted to safer waters after

that. Maera steered them through discussions of the casino, the latest scandal from other worlds, and which nobles were currently feuding over mining rights.

Luisa played her part perfectly, giggling at the right moments and making vapid observations about fashion and jewelry. But Vex could feel the tension radiating from her body where she pressed against his side. After another twenty minutes of careful verbal dancing, Maera finally released them with promises to meet again soon. The knowing gleam in her eyes suggested she thought she had them exactly where she wanted them.

In the elevator, Vex kept a firm grip on Luisa. "What was up in there?"

"Maera's buttering you up to sell a bride profile. I didn't think she'd work that hard just to resell data." She kept her gaze fixed on the display panel, watching floor numbers with striking intensity.

"That's not what I'm talking about." His jaw tightened. She was deflecting, giving him professional assessment when he needed truth.

"Then what?"

"You seemed distracted."

"Don't I have reason to be?" Her eyes flicked to his lips.

"You weren't distracted this morning." The memory hit him hard and fast. Her taste, the way she'd arched beneath his hands, the perfect heat of her body welcoming him home.

Now she was cold. Distant.

"Everything's fine, Vex. Don't worry."

The door opened, and she darted out before he could say more.

He watched her retreat, every instinct screaming that she was lying. Something had spooked her. She was running from more than just the intimacy between them. His dragon stirred restlessly, protective urge warring with the knowledge that she wouldn't welcome his interference. Not yet.

But he was going to find out what was wrong.

15

THIS WAS SO FREAKING STUPID.

Luisa slunk down the hallway outside of the suite and headed for the Frost Lounge at the appointed time. Vex was trying to make a secured call back to his IDA contact and hadn't paid her any mind when she said she was going out.

Good.

She was slipping. He already thought she was off her game, and she wanted to *kill* Brant Tallyer for putting her in this position. If Vex found out she'd screwed up the mission. If he found out about her past …

Why did she even care about that?

So she'd stolen? There was no such thing as crime on Aetis, not in the legal sense. You'd need a government for that. She'd grown up there, come up from the dankest slums, and survived. You couldn't ask for more.

The rationalization felt hollow.

She'd broken into personal systems, violated privacy, destroyed lives with the information she'd uncovered. The kind of work that left stains on your soul that no amount of justification could wash clean.

But she didn't think Vex would see it that way.

She was beginning to suspect the "lord" part of his backstory wasn't made up. He was too comfortable in the role. And the way he'd talked about the estate back on Vemion? That sounded real.

He came from a world of honor and nobility, where people followed codes that meant something. He'd look at her past and see exactly what she was: a gutter rat who'd clawed her way up by stepping on anyone who got in her way.

So what was a real lord doing on this job?

The question piqued her curiosity, but it was the least of her worries.

The casino's corridors seemed different when she was walking them alone. The soft lighting felt oppressive, creating shadows that could hide watching eyes. Every well-dressed patron she passed might be a spy. Her heart rate picked up as she navigated the maze of gaming floors toward the Frost Lounge. The thrum of activity should have been comforting. Instead, it felt like a farce designed to lull people into false security while predators like Tallyer moved freely among them.

The place was nearly deserted. It was too early for pre-dinner drinks and too late for the lunch crowd. There were better views in other bars. This place was just … quiet.

And Brant Tallyer was waiting for her at a secluded table in the back.

He sat in an alcove screened by decorative plants, positioned so anyone sitting there would have a clear view of the entrance while remaining mostly hidden. Tallyer had claimed the chair facing the room's main entrance, forcing her to take the seat with her back to the door. A tactical disadvantage that made her skin crawl.

The air in the Frost Lounge lived up to its name, cooled to an almost uncomfortable degree and scented with something sharp that reminded her of winter mornings in the undercity. Tallyer sat relaxed in his chair, holding a glass of whiskey, looking like a successful businessman enjoying a quiet drink.

But his eyes held the same gleam she remembered, the look of a man who enjoyed having power over others.

"You came," he said, sounding genuinely surprised. "You look different."

"You're not dead." She couldn't think of anything else to say.

He grinned. "Just a little misunderstanding between me and my creditors. You know how it is."

"I left that life behind." Her fingers twitched with the urge to reach for a weapon, not that she ever carried one.

"It looks like! I never thought I'd see you on the arm of some rich man, his pretty bauble. I seem to remember you saying you'd die before you sold your ass to anyone." Why did he sound so jovial?

"I just said that to keep you out of my bed." There was something familiar to the banter, and it made Luisa's skin crawl at how easy it was to slip back into it.

He laughed, a full-throated guffaw that would have attracted attention if there had been anyone else in there. "You've always been special, Lu. I'm glad you've done so well for yourself."

He was buying her cover. Good. He wasn't about to report her and Vex to the casino for arriving under false pretenses. Aetis didn't have laws, sure, but businesses were more than happy to enforce their rules with the judicious application of violence.

"Did you just summon me to catch up?" She didn't have time for reminiscing. Vex would wonder where she was before long.

"I wish it could have been." He sounded genuine. That was the thing about Brant. When you were his friend, on his side, he'd move the stars to protect you.

When you lost that friendship? Or when he decided you were no longer useful?

At one point in her life, Luisa had thought he was the best partner she could hope to have. She did her best to stay on his good side and never earn his ire.

It hadn't mattered a bit.

"What do you want?" she asked.

He answered without shame. "Fifty thousand credits."

"What! I don't have a tenth of that!" The surprise shocked the truth right out of her.

He took a sip of his whiskey before responding. "Your lord keeping you on that tight of a leash? He got you that necklace you were wearing the other night, and that has to be half the worth right there."

"I can't pawn stones my … lover gave to me in the middle of this casino." Was the necklace really that expensive? She'd tried not to think about it.

It further cemented her belief that Vex had to be a real lord. No way did their operating budget allow for extravagant purchases like that.

Brant shrugged. "Then get him to loosen the leash. He has the cash."

"And if I can't get it?" What was he threatening to expose? He knew the worst of her crimes; he'd challenged her to do most of them. And if he tried to sell her out, he had to know that she'd do her best to drag him down with her.

Unless someone was protecting him.

"If not, I tell Maera Daxkar all about your skills, and she'll collar you and use you until you dry up. She'll pay almost as much for you as I'm asking for."

"You'd try and sell me to her?" Bile rose in her throat.

Brant looked almost sorrowful. "But I don't want to do that. Fifty thousand, and this all goes away."

Until the next ask. That's how blackmail worked. Always.

Luisa had to salvage this. "My skills are rusty. Daxkar wouldn't get her money's worth."

Brant stood up and gave her a pitying look. "Oh, Louisa. She will." He walked away.

Panic hit her hard, stealing her breath.

Fifty thousand credits might as well have been fifty million. Her legitimate work paid well, but not enough to cover extortion demands. And Vex … she couldn't even begin to imagine that conversation.

How could she explain why she needed the credits without revealing everything?

Running was an option, but a terrible one. The Mountain sat on an isolated peak, accessible only by air transport. Even if she could get past casino security, where would she go? Back to the undercity where Tallyer's old contacts would find her in no time? Off-planet without any connections? She was trapped.

The worst part was knowing this was just the beginning. Fifty thousand now, but blackmailers never stopped with one payment. He'd bleed her dry. And then he'd sell her to Maera anyway, just because he could.

Her hands started shaking as reality sank in.

Every choice she'd made to build a legitimate life could be undone with a few well-placed words.

Maera already suspected something was off; Tallyer's information would confirm those suspicions and give the woman exactly what she needed to destroy both Luisa and the mission. The thought of being collared, of being used as a tool by someone like Maera until her skills were exhausted and her mind broken, made her sick.

She pressed her fingers against her temples, trying to think through the panic. There had to be an angle. Tallyer was confident, cocky even, but overconfidence had always been his weakness. He thought he held all the cards, but maybe he'd overlooked something.

But what? She had no leverage, no resources he didn't know about. And time was running out. The careful balance she'd been maintaining between past and present was crumbling. The professional competence she'd worked so hard to build felt like a costume slipping away.

She was so caught up in her own head that she didn't hear Vex approach. He slid into the seat that Brant had abandoned.

"Care to tell me what that was about?"

16

LUISA HAD no reason to be meeting with some low life.

The rage that flooded through Vex was irrational and completely beyond his control. Heat built beneath his skin, smoke threatening to curl from his fingertips as he watched her sit across from that piece of scum like they were old friends.

Every instinct screamed at him to intervene, to tear the man apart for daring to even look at her. The possessive thought should have shocked him, but all he could focus on was the way Luisa's shoulders had tensed, the careful way she held herself like she was afraid.

She was supposed to be his partner. She was supposed to trust him enough to come to him if there was trouble. Instead, she'd snuck away like a thief in the night to meet with someone clearly dangerous.

The betrayal cut deeper than it had any right to, considering the length of their partnership.

He'd followed her path through the casino, his dragon senses locked onto her like a tracking beacon. The Frost Lounge had been easy enough to find, and positioning himself where he could hear some of their conversation even easier.

"I was—"

"We're going back to our room." He managed to keep his voice level, controlled, but barely.

The effort of not touching her was monumental. If he put his hands on her right now, he might drag her out of the lounge like some kind of caveman, consequences be damned. She wasn't his to claim, wasn't his to protect, no matter what his dragon insisted.

They were partners. *Temporary* partners. Nothing more.

But the careful distance he maintained as they walked was torture. She moved with that careful grace he'd come to recognize, but there was something fragile about her posture now, something that made the protective instincts rage even harder against his attempts at rational thought.

The elevator ride was silent except for the soft mechanical hum. Vex stared at the floor indicator, watching the numbers climb, and fought the urge to demand answers right there. But everywhere was under fucking surveillance. This conversation needed to happen in the only space they could be certain was private.

Their attendant was nowhere to be seen when they entered the suite, but Vex didn't trust the absence. He guided Luisa straight through to the bedroom, his hand hovering just behind her back without quite touching.

The moment they were inside, he slammed the door behind them with enough force to rattle the frame.

"Don't you dare tell me you were following a lead." He nearly roared it.

"I knew what I was doing." The words came out steady enough, but Vex could see the cracks in her composure. Her hands were clasped tightly in front of her, knuckles white with tension.

"Do you not understand how dangerous this could get?" The question came out rougher than he'd intended, edged with the smoke he was fighting to contain.

"We're dealing with data from a dating agency, not arms dealers." Her voice lacked conviction.

"Data that Maera has made it clear she's willing to use to broker high-level partnerships. Do you think she doesn't have an ulterior motive? Do you think she's working with Tallyer? Is that why you went down there? *Alone*?" The last word came out as almost a growl, his dragon bleeding through despite his best efforts to maintain control.

"No."

"Want to tell me why then? We're partners, we need to trust each other." The word "partners" felt inadequate, insufficient to describe whatever this thing between them had become. But it was all he could safely offer.

"Like I know anything about you!"

The accusation hit him in the chest, unexpected and sharp enough to cut through his anger. For a moment, he was thrown completely off balance. He'd kept his cards close to his chest, revealed only what was necessary for the mission.

But that was just the way he operated.

"I haven't hidden anything from you. You know

who I am, why I'm here." But even as he said it, it felt somewhat hollow.

"Then what's an actual lord doing working this job? Don't you have peasants to annoy or something?" There was bite in her voice now, defensive anger that made her stand straighter, chin lifted in challenge.

Old aristocratic arrogance came easily, a shield against the uncomfortable truth in her words. "The peasants annoy themselves just fine. I've never hidden my title."

"You didn't make it obvious either."

They were circling each other now, the space between them charged with more than just anger. There were layers to this fight, undercurrents he could feel but not quite identify.

Everything was rising to the surface now, all the careful distance they'd maintained crumbling under the weight of emotions neither of them was prepared to acknowledge. Her cheeks were flushed with color, her breathing slightly uneven, and despite his fury, Vex found himself noting the way her dress hugged her curves, the way her hair had come slightly loose from its careful arrangement.

This was about more than the mission. More than her meeting with Tallyer. This was about trust and betrayal and the way she'd looked at him last night like he might actually matter. The way he'd gone to sleep with her in his arms and felt like he'd found something he hadn't even known he was looking for.

But beneath it all was the knowledge that she was in danger, and she hadn't trusted him enough to ask for help.

"So what didn't *you* make obvious? Why is Brant Tallyer meeting with you and threatening you?" He had to get some control back.

She went completely still, her face draining of color as she realized exactly how much he'd overheard. The fear that flickered across her features made his protective instincts roar, momentarily overwhelming the anger in a way that left him feeling unsteady.

"He said he'd sell you to Maera Daxkar. If he thought you were really mine, he wouldn't dare."

The words *really mine* hung in the air. The thought of anyone laying claim to her, of anyone using her skills until there was nothing left of the brilliant, fierce woman he'd come to care about far too much, made smoke curl around him.

It was like she was being held up by strings that were suddenly cut. Luisa sagged and sat on the bed.

"Where do you think I learned to do what I do?" Her voice was small now, defeated in a way that made his chest ache.

"What?" The single word came out too sharp.

"Hacking complex systems? Scanning data? Everything I've done over the last few days, do you think there's some kind of, I don't know, college on Aetis that teaches it?" There was bitter humor in her voice now, self-deprecating in a way that made him want to cross the room and pull her into his arms.

"The IDA said you were the best." He was struggling to process what she was telling him.

"I *am* the best. Because Brant Tallyer took me under his wing when I was sixteen and hooked me up with some of the most vicious hackers and data brokers in the quadrant."

It hurt to hear it.

Of course she was a criminal. How else would someone develop the kind of skills she possessed? But knowing it intellectually and hearing her say it out loud were two different things entirely. The woman who'd taken him apart with her hands and her mouth and her brilliant mind, was a thief. Had always been a thief.

And then he was angry at himself for being shocked.

What had he expected? Some pristine princess who'd learned hacking as a hobby? The underworld didn't produce people like Luisa by accident. It forged them in fire and desperation, and the fact that she'd survived it, had thrived enough to be sitting here with him now, should have impressed him.

Instead, all he could think about was how she'd deceived him, how she'd let him believe she was something she wasn't.

The anger came roaring back, hotter and more dangerous than before. She'd lied to him. Maybe not directly, but by omission, and that felt like betrayal in a way that made rational thought nearly impossible.

"So Tallyer is your ex?" The question came out tight, controlled, but he could hear the edge of violence underneath.

She made an almost comically horrified face. "Absolutely not! I'd never touch that slimy toad." The disgust in her voice was genuine and immediate.

His dragon was satisfied with that answer, at least. And that only made Vex angrier.

"He wants fifty grand, or he'll sell me to Maera for my skills. He still thinks I'm your pretty bauble. Our cover is intact. We can fix this." She was trying to sound professional, competent, but he could hear the fear underneath.

"How the fuck do you think I can trust you after this?" The words came out cruel, designed to hurt, and he saw them land hard. Part of him immediately wanted to take them back, but the larger part of him was too angry, too betrayed to care about the pain that flickered across her features.

"Just because I didn't tell you doesn't mean I lied. I'm here to do the job." But her voice was smaller now, less certain.

"Or are you here to rob the casino blind?" The accusation was unfair, and he knew it, but he couldn't seem to stop himself.

"What? No! And who would care if I did? It's a bunch of rich assholes. But I haven't touched anything but their outer security. The money's better protected than that." There was heat in her voice again, defensive anger that made her eyes flash.

"How would you know?" He was being deliberately obtuse now, pushing for a reaction.

"Because it's a fucking casino. They're all like

that." Exasperation colored her tone, like she was explaining something obvious to a child.

"Have you tried to rob the Mountain before?" The question was a trap.

Her answer came fast, automatic. "No!"

"Don't lie to me." His voice had gone dangerously quiet.

"I'm not. It would be too difficult to ever try. There are much easier targets."

The casual way she said it, like robbery was just another career option to consider, made his vision go red around the edges. She wasn't even trying to pretend she was reformed, wasn't making any excuses or apologies for what she'd done.

"You're done with this job." The words came out absolute.

"You don't have the authority to do that. You need me." But there was desperation creeping into her voice now, like she was starting to realize how serious he was.

"I need a partner I can trust. And I can't trust you. When does Tallyer expect the money?" Each word was carefully controlled, but underneath was a fury that threatened to burn everything in its path.

"Oh, so you're going to pay him?" Hope flickered in her voice, quickly followed by confusion.

"No."

The single word seemed to drain what little fight she had left. Her shoulders sagged, and for a moment, she looked younger, more vulnerable, like the sixteen-year-old girl who'd been desperate enough to throw in with a man like Tallyer.

"He didn't say," she admitted.

He had to do what he could to salvage this. "I'll get you transport to the city. Disappear. It's the least you can do."

17

VEX WOULDN'T TALK to her. He wouldn't even look at her.

The silence in their suite pressed against her chest with every breath. Luisa had never been ashamed of her past, of doing what she needed to survive. Survival didn't come with a moral handbook on Aetis. You took what opportunities presented themselves, or you starved in the undercity's gutters.

But lying to Vex? That felt wrong on a level she couldn't articulate.

Three hours since he'd stormed out, his final words echoing: "Don't ruin anything else." Three hours of pacing marble floors while their attendant moved through his duties with careful indifference, as if her world hadn't just imploded.

Vex had returned once, briefly, shoulders rigid as he'd activated the communication system. She'd caught fragments through the bedroom door, transport arrangements, departure times. He was getting her off the Mountain, away from Tallyer's threats.

Why was he protecting her? After everything she'd hidden, after manipulating him into bed to avoid his questions, why arrange her safe passage? It would be easier to let Tallyer have her. But instead, he was ensuring her safety while cutting her out of his life.

Was he really protecting her? Or the job?

One night in his arms had completely messed her up. The memory burned through her, the way he'd whispered her name like a prayer, hands mapping every inch of her skin.

She'd felt claimed beyond the physical, marked by something deeper than desire. The connection had been electric, like two shards of broken glass fitting together perfectly. For those brief hours, she'd belonged to someone who saw her as more than just a tool.

But it was as much a lie as her life.

She had to fix this.

The need drove her to her feet. She wouldn't leave branded as the criminal who'd sabotaged their mission. She was the best hacker in three systems, and she'd prove it.

Vex needed a clear connection between Maera Daxkar and the IDA data. Maera was dangling hope of some perfect match so he'd pay an exorbitant amount for his bride.

But where was she storing the data? And how had she gotten it?

The question pulled her to her equipment. The data she'd harvested scrolled across the screen: financial records, communication logs, transaction histories. All circumstantial. The real proof would be buried deeper, in systems requiring physical access.

The Mountain's private servers.

They'd be housed in secure levels below the casino floor, protected by digital and physical security. But she'd memorized the building's layout, the service corridors and maintenance access points. If she could reach the server room, she could plug directly into their network backbone.

She could fix this.

Luisa selected her outfit with precision. The midnight blue evening dress suggested she belonged in exclusive spaces. Matching heels added confidence, transforming her from nervous hacker into wealthy patron. She swept her hair up, applied makeup, and slipped Vex's emerald necklace around her throat.

The transformation was complete. Anyone who saw her would see a rich man's beautiful companion, slightly drunk on champagne and exploring where she shouldn't.

Harmless. Forgettable.

And if Vex saw her and felt regret? Well ... Good.

The casino floor buzzed with evening energy. Luisa moved through crowds with ease, smile bright and vacant. A few heads turned thanks to the dress, but no one paid undue attention.

The employee corridor was tucked behind a service alcove, entrance disguised by decorative paneling. She slipped inside, footsteps muffled as she descended toward the secure levels.

She pulled her portable interface from her evening bag, connecting it to the lock pad's data port. The familiar steps centered her, focused her mind on the elegant puzzle of the Mountain's defenses.

She was in.

The server room hummed with quiet energy, banks of processing units creating a maze of blinking lights. This was the Mountain's digital heart. She found an access terminal and connected her equipment, losing herself in the dance of code and countermeasure.

Maera's private files were encrypted, but not beyond her skills. Layer by layer, Luisa peeled back the protection. Financial records showing payments from data brokers. Communication logs with buyers interested in purchasing romantic profiles. And then she found a directory marked with the IDA's encrypted signature, containing files that should never have left their secure servers.

Proof.

Luisa typed a command on her keyboard, executing a code right as the door opened with a hiss. "What are you doing in here?" Zymon, Maera's personal security guard, demanded.

Luisa whipped around, her mind scrambling for an excuse.

But Zymon looked at her with narrowed eyes. "Maera said there was something off with you."

He raised his hand and fired his blaster.

Everything went black.

18

ANOTHER THOUSAND CREDITS LOST.

The chips clattered against the felt as Vex pushed them forward. Around him, soft murmurs mixed with distant slot machine chimes from the main casino floor. This was the first time since arriving that he was actually losing.

He didn't care.

The cards might as well have been blank. Every number, every suit blurred as his mind replayed the confrontation in their suite. Luisa's voice, small and defeated, admitting to a past she'd hidden. The way she'd looked when he'd told her she was done, like he'd struck her.

Luisa was a liar. A thief.

Rage and hurt clawed at his chest. The betrayal burned through every moment of trust they'd built. Every breathless sound she'd made beneath him— had any of it been real? Or had she been manipulating him the same way she manipulated security systems?

She'd used him, let him believe she was something she wasn't. The memory of her hands on his skin, the way she'd whispered his name, now felt tainted.

And why did he care so much?

He'd worked with dozens of operatives over the years. Professional partnerships were exactly that— professional. When they ended, he walked away without a backward glance.

She wasn't his first partner. She wasn't even the first one to betray him.

Did she really betray you? a voice in his head asked. It sounded suspiciously like his mother's calm tone.

Yes.

But had she?

His rational mind began picking apart his anger. He wasn't owed every detail of her past. She didn't know his details either—that he was an operative for his king. He'd never considered telling her.

Would he have said something if he'd met someone who might compromise the mission?

A player across the table laughed, the sound grating against his nerves. He shoved more chips forward.

He didn't know.

The cards were dealt, but Vex barely registered them. His thoughts churned, anger and guilt and longing fighting for dominance. Maybe she'd just been trying to survive, the same way he'd been trying to complete his mission.

She hadn't chosen her past any more than he'd chosen his noble blood. Yet the hurt remained, because, somewhere in the last few days, he'd started thinking of her as ... more. Not just his partner or temporary lover, but as someone he wanted to keep.

Who was Luisa to him, anyway? They barely knew each other. Once he sent her home, he'd never see her again.

No.

The word echoed with absolute certainty. His dragon stirred beneath his skin at the thought of her facing danger alone. Whatever was between them, he couldn't just walk away. Couldn't send her back to a life where people like Tallyer could threaten her.

Damn it.

A cheer went up around the table as he lost again.

The celebration felt distant. His fingers drummed against the table, matching the agitation in his chest.

Maera Daxkar slid into the chair beside him, a pink drink in her hand. She gave him her shark's smile. "A bit of a losing streak, my lord?"

He folded. "The cards give, and the cards take away."

"That they do." She sipped her drink, eyes never leaving his face. Something flickered in her expression. "Now that you're away from your lovely companion, I thought we could talk. It's so hard to plan for your future when the past is sitting on your lap." Her smile sharpened.

Alarm bells sounded in his head. "She's in our rooms. My bed. Doing as she's told."

If only any of that were true.

"Is she?" Maera drained her glass and set it down with a soft clink.

Ice flooded Vex's veins. Maera's tone held the satisfied purr of someone who knew where all the pieces were positioned. She wouldn't be here making veiled threats unless she had leverage.

He didn't have time for her games.

He gathered his chips with practiced efficiency. Nothing else mattered now. Not when his dragon was roaring for him to find her, protect her, regardless of what secrets she'd kept.

He cashed out and stood. "Duty calls, I'm afraid. Perhaps we can continue our conversation another time."

Maera's smile never wavered, but her gaze was hungry. "Of course, my lord. I'm sure we'll have plenty to discuss very soon."

The words followed him toward the elevators, each step controlled despite the urgency clawing at his chest. The casino floor blurred around him. His senses strained for any trace of her, but recycled air and mingled perfumes obscured everything.

Maera might have just been testing him, but Vex didn't care.

The elevator took forever to arrive. Tallyer could have found her. Maera's security could have taken her. She could be bleeding somewhere while he'd been nursing his wounded pride.

If there was even a chance that Luisa was in danger, he was going to protect her.

The elevator doors opened, and he stepped inside. For the first time since he'd stormed out of their suite, his purpose was crystal clear. Whatever had happened between them, none of it mattered as much as keeping her safe.

He couldn't do anything else.

19

IT WAS COLD. Freezing. Blistering.

Brisk.

The words cycled through Luisa's sluggish mind as consciousness crept back in fragments. Her skull throbbed where Zymon's blaster had struck her, a sharp counterpoint to the bone-deep ache radiating from everywhere at once.

Luisa shivered as she sat up, her evening gown and heels useless against the chill. The midnight blue fabric that had made her feel confident in the casino now clung in icy sheets, offering no protection against wind that cut through silk like a blade. Snow accumulated in the folds of her skirt, and her bare arms were mottled red and white. The emerald necklace Vex had given her felt like a glacier around her throat.

She'd been dumped in the cold. Snow fell in thick, lazy flakes that would have been beautiful under other circumstances. Now they felt like frozen daggers against her exposed skin.

The Haddiac Mountains rolled on in every direction. Luisa squinted against the blowing snow but couldn't make out lights from the casino.

This was how they disposed of people. The realization hit her with absolute clarity. No messy murders in pristine corridors, no blood on expensive carpets, no bodies to explain to guests. Just dump the problems outside and let the mountain do the work. Clean. Efficient. Deniable.

The wind howled around the peaks like something alive and hungry, carrying the promise of slow, frozen death. How many others had Maera's people taken there? The mountain would claim her bones like it had claimed so many others, leaving nothing but another mysterious disappearance to file away and forget.

A low growl echoed from the darkness beyond the tree line, followed by the crunch of something large moving through snow. Luisa's blood turned to ice as she realized she wasn't alone on this desolate peak. Whatever lived up here would smell her fear, her blood, her vulnerability.

The cold might kill her slowly, but the local wildlife would be faster.

Panic shot through her, burning away the sluggish haze clouding her thoughts. She refused to be dinner for some beast.

Her legs were numb blocks as she tried to stand, pins and needles shooting through her calves as circulation returned. The heels that had made her feel elegant in the casino were death traps now, their thin soles providing no traction on icy rock. She kicked them off without hesitation, the expensive shoes disappearing into snow.

The cold bit into her bare feet immediately, sharp enough to make her gasp. But she could feel the ground, sense the subtle variations that might mean the difference between solid footing and a fatal fall. She stumbled forward through drifts, her dress tangling around her legs.

Through a gap in swirling snow, she glimpsed lights twinkling in the distance. The casino, still perched on its impossible peak like a glittering jewel against the storm. It looked impossibly far away, but she was definitely on the same mountain. The lights flickered through snow, but they were real.

A destination she could reach if she kept moving.

Hope flared, warm and desperate. She wasn't going to die on this ledge. Not when Vex was still in danger, not when the mission hung in the balance. Maera might have thought she was disposing of a problem, but she'd underestimated exactly how hard Luisa was to kill.

She began trudging through snow, following what might have been an animal path. Each step was a battle against wind that tried to knock her sideways, against snow that filled her tracks almost as fast as she could make them. Her thoughts grew sluggish as cold crept deeper into her bones, making it harder to focus on the distant lights. The silk of her dress had frozen stiff in places, cracking when she moved and letting wind find new places to torment her skin.

Her fingers had gone completely numb, making it impossible to gather the dress properly. The fabric caught on every branch and rock, tearing in places that let even more cold reach her skin. But she kept moving, driven by stubborn will and the knowledge that stopping meant dying.

She wasn't going to make it much longer.

The realization crept through her mind with the

same inexorable certainty as cold seeping into her bones. Her body was already shutting down non-essential functions, drawing blood away from her extremities to protect vital organs. Soon, she'd start getting clumsy, making mistakes that would send her tumbling off the mountain path. It wouldn't be long after that.

Oh, please, Vex, I'm out here. She didn't have the energy to speak it.

The words formed in her mind like a prayer, too desperate to hold back. She tried to picture his face, the way his eyes had looked when he'd touched her, when he'd whispered her name like something precious.

Would he even notice she was gone? Or would he assume she'd taken the transport he'd arranged and disappeared into whatever new life waited for her?

How would he know? And why would he care?

He'd made his feelings clear back in their suite. She was a liar, a thief, someone he couldn't trust. The passionate man who'd claimed her body with world-shattering intensity had looked at her with cold dismissal when he'd learned the truth about her past.

Why would he waste time looking for someone who'd already betrayed him?

But even as the logical part of her mind accepted that reality, her heart rebelled. What they'd shared had been real, regardless of the secrets she'd kept.

He was in danger, too. Zymon had caught her. He'd know Vex was up to something. And if Zymon knew, Maera would soon.

The thought cut through her self-pity like a blade. While she'd been wallowing in cold and feeling sorry for herself, Vex was walking into a trap he didn't know existed. Maera had all the pieces now, everything she needed to destroy whatever cover story they'd built.

And Vex, with his arrogant assumption that he could handle anything, would never see it coming.

They were going to kill him.

How did you kill a dragon?

The question terrified her more than her own impending death. Dragons were supposed to be nearly indestructible. But Maera's operation was sophisticated, well-funded. If anyone had access to weapons that could take down a dragon lord, it would be someone like her. And Vex, sitting in that casino thinking he was in control, would be completely vulnerable.

She had to warn him. Had to find some way to get word to him before Maera made her move. The data she'd stolen from the server room wouldn't matter if Vex was dead, and all her sacrifice would be meaningless.

Vex, she thought again. Desperately.

She closed her eyes against stinging snow and tried to remember the moment when they'd flown to the casino together. The strange sensation she'd felt when his dragon had communicated with her, that brief connection that had felt like touching something vast and utterly alien.

Could dragons hear thoughts? Somehow?

The idea was ridiculous, desperate, probably just hypothermia starting to affect her judgment. But she had nothing else left to try.

Vex.

20

VEX SLAMMED into the suite like a meteor.

The ornate double doors slammed against the walls with enough force to crack the marble, sound echoed through the empty space. His chest heaved as he swept his gaze across the room, every sense straining for any trace of Luisa's presence.

It was empty. No Luisa. No attendant.

The silence pressed against his eardrums, unnatural and wrong. Her scent lingered faintly, but it was old, growing fainter by the moment. The suite's perfect climate control couldn't mask the absence of her warmth.

The place was pristine. There hadn't been a struggle. If someone had snatched Luisa, they'd done it before she could fight.

Which meant they'd taken her by surprise. Or worse, they'd convinced her to come willingly, luring her into whatever trap they'd set. The thought made his vision blur red around the edges.

Rage roared through him.

Vex tore through the suite like a man possessed, overturning furniture with inhuman strength. The elegant sofa crashed into the wall, its expensive fabric tearing as he searched behind it.

He ripped cushions from chairs, swept ornaments from tables with enough force to shatter them against the floor. The dining table went next, flipping end over end as he checked beneath it.

But the pristine bedroom mocked him with its perfect order. The bed they'd shared, still rumpled from their bodies, sat empty. Her equipment was gone from the table. Even her scent was fading, replaced by the sterile smell of recycled air and expensive furnishings. The dress she'd worn the night before was missing from where she'd draped it over the chair.

Movement in the doorway made him spin around, every muscle coiled for violence. Zymon stood there with three other security guards, their uniforms crisp and their weapons drawn. They moved with the coordinated precision of professionals, spreading out to block his escape routes. Vex catalogued their positions automatically, two by the door, one covering the windows, Zymon in the center with his hand resting on what looked like a military-grade blaster.

"Your woman had to check out early," Zymon said. "And Maera wants to talk to you. Now."

The casual way he said it, like Luisa was just another piece of luggage to be moved around, made heat build beneath his skin, smoke beginning to curl around him as his dragon clawed for release.

The guards rushed him all at once, a coordinated assault designed to overwhelm through sheer numbers. Vex let his fire loose in a burst, the flames washing over two of them before they could react. Their screams filled the air as they stumbled backward, their expensive uniforms catching fire.

But Zymon and the remaining guard had activated personal shields, energy fields that shimmered around them like heat mirages. Vex's fire hit the barriers and dissipated harmlessly, the flames flowing around them like water around stones.

Military-grade protection, the kind that cost more than most people made in a lifetime.

Zymon and his underling backed him toward the massive windows that looked out over the mountains, their movements coordinated and patient. The glass behind him was reinforced, designed to withstand the mountain's fierce weather, but Vex could feel the cold radiating through it.

"You need to come with us now," said Zymon.

"I don't think so." Vex let his transformation begin, his human form expanding and shifting as scales erupted across his skin.

The suite suddenly felt impossibly small as his dragon form took shape, wings scraping against the ceiling. Without hesitation, he launched himself backward, his massive bulk shattering the reinforced window in an explosion of glass and twisted metal. The mountain wind hit him hard, but his wings caught the air current and lifted him away from the casino's facade.

Blaster fire followed him, the energy bolts sparking harmlessly off his scales.

Vex! Luisa's voice screamed in his head.

The telepathic cry screamed through his mind, so clear and desperate that he nearly lost altitude. His dragon brain reeled, trying to process it. Humans couldn't communicate telepathically.

Impossible.

He let instinct guide his flight pattern. His senses swept the mountainside below, searching for any sign of movement against the pristine white landscape. The snow fell in thick sheets, reducing visibility to mere meters in some places.

He flew south of the casino to where the last of the trees died off as it got too cold for them to grow any higher. The landscape below was a study in desolation, nothing but jagged rocks and endless white stretching toward the horizon. Wind howled between the peaks with enough force to ground most aircraft.

But there, a splash of midnight blue against the snow, moving with the desperate, unsteady gait of someone fighting the cold. Even from this distance, he could see her stumbling through the drifts, her evening dress a ridiculous splash of color in the wilderness.

Vex, please, the voice in his head was fainter now, and the figure on the ground stumbled.

Luisa wasn't going to make it much longer. Especially not if the guards on snow mobiles made it to her first.

Three vehicles crested the ridge behind her, their engines whining as they navigated the treacherous terrain. They moved with purpose, clearly tracking her footprints through the snow. The lead rider raised something that looked like a rifle, taking aim at Luisa's struggling form.

Rage flared through him. They were too close to her for him to safely use his fire without hitting her.

She's talking in your head. You know what that means.

The realization crashed over him with the force of absolute truth. The telepathic bond was real, had always been real, and Luisa was speaking to him across the void with the desperate clarity of someone facing death.

There was only one way a human would be able to communicate with him like that.

Unless he was imagining it.

No.

The guards on the snow mobiles were almost on her now.

Vex let his fire loose, watching it wash over the guards and Luisa, whose scream rent the air as it hit her.

And flowed safely around her, not doing her a bit of harm.

The flames engulfed everything in their path, turning the snow to steam and the guards to ash in seconds. But around Luisa, the fire parted like a curtain, creating a perfect circle of safety in the inferno. She stood untouched in the center of the destruction, staring up at him with wide, disbelieving eyes.

His fire could not harm his mate.

Vex circled once, scanning for additional threats, before spiraling down to land near her. His massive dragon form settled into the snow, wings folded against his sides as he lowered his head to meet her gaze.

Up close, he could see the damage the cold had done—her lips were blue, her skin mottled white and red from frostbite, and she was shivering so violently she could barely stand.

Climb on, he thought at her.

The mental connection felt as natural as breathing now that he'd acknowledged it. He could sense her confusion, her disbelief, the way her logical mind was trying to process what had just happened. But beneath it all was relief so profound it would have brought him to his knees if he were in his other form.

She approached him on unsteady legs, her bare feet leaving bloody prints in the snow. The sight of her pain sent fresh rage coursing through his system, but he held perfectly still as she reached for the ridge of scales along his leg. Her fingers had to be numb with cold, making her grip clumsy, but she managed to haul herself up onto his back.

He could feel her fear through their bond, the way she fought to stay conscious as her body finally began to warm against his hide. Her grip on his scales was the desperate hold of someone who'd been seconds from death, and he sent waves of reassurance through their mental link.

Vex launched himself skyward with powerful wingbeats, carrying his precious cargo toward the casino's lights. The storm fought him every meter of the way, wind shear threatening to knock them from the sky, but his dragon form was built for this. He climbed above the worst of the weather, giving Luisa a view of the Mountain from an angle no human was meant to see.

Movement on the roof caught his attention. A sleek speeder sat on the landing pad, its engines already spinning up for departure.

Two figures ran toward it with the desperate haste of people whose plans had just gone catastrophically wrong. Even from this distance, he could make out Maera's distinctive silhouette and Zymon's bulk beside her.

Vex folded his wings and dove, the speeder growing larger in his vision with each passing second. He could incinerate them both where they stood, end this threat to his mate with a single burst of dragonfire.

But he still had a mission to complete. The stolen IDA data was somewhere in this building and destroying it along with Maera would leave too many questions unanswered.

He targeted the speeder instead, letting his fire loose in a concentrated stream that turned the vehicle into slag. The explosion sent both figures diving for cover, their escape route eliminated in a burst of superheated metal and burning fuel.

He landed and let Luisa carefully climb off before transforming back to his human form.

The change was swift, his dragon form condensing back into human shape. But he kept his fire ready, flames dancing around his fingers as he stalked toward the two figures cowering behind the wreckage of their transport. Maera's perfect composure had finally cracked, her face white with terror.

Vex held his fire in his palm, staring Maera down.

The flames cast dancing shadows across the rooftop, their heat turning the falling snow to steam around his hand. He could end this now. One gesture, one moment of released fury, and the woman who'd tried to kill his mate would be nothing but ash on the wind.

But even through the haze of protective rage, his tactical mind asserted itself. Maera knew things about the data theft, about her buyers, about the larger network that had made this operation possible. Dead criminals told no tales, and there were still questions that needed answers.

He closed his fist and let the fire disappear. He still had a job to do.

"Let's talk."

21

LUISA WAS PRETTY sure she was on fire somewhere, burning to a crisp in dragon-induced death after Vex let it rip. All of this? A pre-death hallucination that would end any second as her last synapses fired.

Any second now.

No?

The cold mountain air bit at her exposed skin, sharp and real. Her bare feet stung against the snow-covered rooftop, and the silk of her ruined evening gown clung to her like ice. She was alive. Impossibly, miraculously alive, standing in the aftermath of dragonfire that should have reduced her to ash.

Maera Daxkar stood next to Zymon and the

smoldering wreckage of her speeder. She didn't look like a woman whose escape was cut off. She was smiling.

Luisa really didn't like that.

"It's over, Maera," Vex said. His voice was steely fury. He was pissed, and smoke was coming off of him in waves. "Surrender yourself to my custody, agree to testify against your co-conspirators, and you'll get some leniency."

Maera's smile widened, revealing teeth that looked too sharp in the emergency lighting from the burning speeder. She straightened her jacket with deliberate calm, as if facing down an enraged dragon lord was just another business meeting.

Zymon shifted beside her, his hand moving toward his weapon, but Maera raised one finger, and he froze. The woman had nerves of steel. But there was something in her eyes, a glittering confidence that suggested she wasn't nearly as trapped as she appeared.

"You can't touch me without violating the casino rules, Lord Vex." Her voice carried the smooth certainty of someone who'd built a career on knowing exactly which laws applied when.

"Those rules ceased to matter the moment you tried to kill my mate." The word came out as a growl, and fresh smoke curled from his fingertips. The temperature around him spiked, turning the falling snow to steam.

His mate? Where?

He reached out and took her hand, squeezing it. *Her?*

The contact sent electricity shooting up her arm, warm and impossible. His palm was furnace-hot against her frozen fingers, and she could feel something deeper in the touch, a connection that hummed beneath her skin like a live wire. Her logical mind reeled, trying to process what he'd just claimed, but her body seemed to already know the truth.

What Luisa felt went far beyond confusion, but she tried to keep her face neutral. Answers were for later, when Maera Daxkar wasn't on the edge of getting away with everything.

Maera's expression faltered for only a moment. "We can work something out here. That data could make us both rich beyond your wildest dreams."

"I don't need money." The dismissal was so absolute, so casual, that it drove home just how different their worlds really were.

"And the data's gone," Luisa added, her mind catching up a bit and feeling triumphant. It didn't counterbalance the unsteadiness caused by Vex's declaration.

Mate.

What the hell.

Maera froze. The color drained from her face, leaving her looking waxen in the orange glow of the burning transport. Zymon's head snapped toward her, his expression shifting from professional calm to barely contained panic. For the first time since Luisa had met her, Maera looked genuinely rattled.

"You never had access to that data," Maera sneered.

"Your man found me in the private servers. I corrupted that data ten minutes before he got to me." The words came easily, delivered with practiced confidence.

"Then why were you still there?" Zymon demanded.

"Because I was doing a thorough job." She met his gaze without flinching.

In one fluid motion, Zymon drew his blaster and leveled it at her chest. The weapon hummed to life, its energy coils glowing with lethal intent. Vex's response was instant—fire erupted around his hands as he stepped directly in front of Luisa, blocking her from the line of fire.

"You're not getting away," said Vex. "But I can make this easier for you."

"After what happened to your precious mate?" Maera scoffed. "I'm not an idiot."

And there was that word again.

The standoff stretched between them. Zymon's finger hovered over the trigger while Vex's flames danced higher, casting writhing shadows across the rooftop. The wind howled around them, carrying the acrid smell of burning metal and whatever chemicals went into making a speeder all speedy.

Mechanical whirring cut through the tension.

Half a dozen security drones materialized from the storm, their sleek forms circling the rooftop with military precision. Red targeting beams swept across the snow, painting everyone in crimson light.

From the way Maera took cover behind Zymon, these drones weren't hers.

The door to the roof's stairwell opened, and Jaekob Kaur, the Mountain's concierge, stepped out. His uniform was perfectly pressed, and he looked ready to settle a dinner dispute, not step between an angry dragon and a criminal.

"This will not do," said the concierge.

"He broke neutrality!" Maera yelled, pointing at Vex from behind Zymon's broad back.

Vex let his fire dissipate but didn't respond. Instead, he waited a beat before speaking. "Maera Daxkar has been operating an illegal data brokering operation out of your facility. I have been tasked with stopping it."

Kaur's expression remained perfectly neutral, the practiced indifference of someone who'd spent years managing the affairs of the wealthy and dangerous. He surveyed the burning wreckage and armed standoff with the same calm efficiency he might use to assess a dinner reservation conflict.

"What our guests do is their own business," said Kaur. "But we do not tolerate violence."

"I only acted in self-defense," said Vex. "And I believe that is allowed."

The concierge nodded.

"He's lying!" Maera objected.

"Then give me your version of events," Kaur offered. "I'm sure we can come to a reasonable agreement here."

A bribe. Or something like it.

Luisa recognized a man looking for payment. And this was Aetis, after all. No one was clean.

"I'll cut you in on the operation," Maera offered desperately. "One third—no, half!—of all my fees. That's surely more than your salary." Clearly, she didn't believe Luisa had destroyed the data. Or she was bluffing.

If she was, she was good.

Kaur turned to Vex with a raised eyebrow.

Vex's response was bland. "My uncle is the king of Vemion. What do you want?"

Maera's composure finally cracked completely. She spat curses in three different languages, her voice rising to a shriek that cut through the wind. Zymon tried to pull her back, but she shook him off, her face twisted with rage.

"Some of our guests have had trouble in your air space. It's becoming an issue." Kaur's tone was conversational, as if they were discussing catering options rather than negotiating over a criminal's fate.

"We don't let slavers through." Vex was firm.

"No, I wouldn't ask that."

Vex's voice carried the casual authority of someone accustomed to making deals that affected entire star systems. "Then we can work something out. A security passcode you can offer your guests for safe transit?"

"Done."

All of the drones turned to face Maera and Zymon.

"This is not how things are done here!" she yelled.

The concierge gave her a concerned look. "Of course it is." He turned to Vex. "Shall I take care of this for you?"

Vex considered it. Then he shook his head. "Put her in custody. I'll have a transport come for her and remand them into IDA custody."

"Consider it done."

Vex held out a hand, and Luisa took it.

His fingers intertwined with hers, warm and solid and real. The simple contact grounded her, cutting through the surreal chaos of the last few hours. The job was over. They'd won. Maera's operation was finished, the stolen data destroyed, and somehow, impossibly, they were both still alive.

The job was over.

But he had a fuckload of explaining to do.

22

LUISA WAS WAITING for any of this to make sense.

The events of the last few hours felt like fragments of someone else's life. Her mind kept trying to process it all in logical sequence, but every time she reached the part where he'd called her his mate, her thoughts scattered.

Apparently, their suite was a disaster of broken glass and blood, so she and Vex had been given a different suite on a different floor. Smaller, but perfectly functional.

The new accommodations were elegant, cream-colored walls, expensive furniture that managed to look both luxurious and understated, and floor-to-ceiling windows that offered a breathtaking view of the mountain peaks. But Luisa barely noticed the decor.

Her entire focus had narrowed to the man who couldn't seem to stay still, who kept looking at her like she might disappear if he blinked.

Vex had draped his jacket over her shoulders, and every time she even *thought* about shrugging it off, she heard a growl in the back of his throat and pulled the lapels tighter.

The fabric still held his warmth, along with his scent—something clean and masculine with an underlying hint of smoke that reminded her exactly what he was. The weight of it around her shoulders felt like a claim, protective and possessive in equal measure. She should have found it annoying, this casual assumption of ownership, but instead, it made something deep in her chest flutter.

He'd lit the fire with a negligent flick of his fingers, sending a ball of flame into the massive fireplace.

Okay, that was impressive.

The casual display of power should have been terrifying. But she found herself fascinated by the fluid grace of the gesture, the way fire responded to his will like an extension of his body. This was what he really was beneath the expensive clothes and aristocratic manners, something powerful that could reduce the casino to ash without breaking a sweat. And he'd used that power to save her.

There hadn't been a room attendant when they got to the room, thankfully. Apparently, the Mountain was done spying on them.

The absence felt strange after days of constant surveillance, like a weight had been lifted. No more careful performances, no more coded conversations designed to mislead eavesdropping ears. Just the two of them and the truth hanging between them like a sword.

Or she was fooling herself and the room was chalk full of bugs.

Luisa's hands were still shaking with the adrenaline come-down, and she didn't have it in her to find her scanner and sweep the room.

Her fingers trembled as she pulled his jacket tighter, the fine tremor a reminder of how close she'd come to dying out there. Death had been minutes away, maybe less, and only Vex's intervention had saved her.

What did it matter? Their covers were blown. They'd won the day.

And Vex said she was his *mate*.

The word echoed in her mind with the weight

of absolute certainty, as if something fundamental about the universe had shifted and she was still trying to catch up.

Mate.

Not girlfriend, not lover, not partner.

Mate.

Like they were two halves of something that had been split apart and was finally whole again.

That still didn't make sense.

"How?" Her voice was almost swallowed by the crackling of the fire.

Vex moved through the sitting area like a caged predator, his usual composed control replaced by restless energy that made the air itself feel charged. He kept glancing at her, his eyes tracking her every movement, and she could see the tension in the rigid line of his shoulders.

Everything about his posture suggested a man who wanted nothing more than to cross the room and gather her into his arms, but something was holding him back.

The space between them felt impossible to bridge, charged with too much emotion and too many unspoken truths. Luisa drew her legs up onto the sofa, making herself smaller. She felt fragile, like the wrong word or gesture might shatter her completely.

"I thought you were going to kill me," she said, "when you found me outside. I saw your fire coming, and I was sure that was the end."

"I knew it wouldn't harm you." The certainty in his voice was absolute, unshakeable, like he was stating a fundamental law of physics.

"But *how*?" She pushed herself up from the sofa, driven by nervous energy, then immediately sank back down as her legs proved too unsteady to support her.

"I could hear your thoughts in my mind. There is only one human in the universe that could be true for. And my fire cannot harm my mate."

My mate.

How could he say it so simply?

"So just like that, everything's forgiven? Fate points the finger at me, and you're not pissed anymore that I lied to you?" The words came out sharper than she'd intended, edged with fury. The memory of his cold dismissal in their original suite burned in her chest, the way he'd looked at her like she was something distasteful he needed to scrape off his boot.

How dare he stand there looking at her with

warm eyes when just hours ago he'd been ready to ship her off Aetis like trash?

"You were in an impossible situation, and I regretted my reaction almost as soon as you left. If I hadn't been an idiot, you wouldn't have almost died out there." His voice carried the weight of genuine remorse, and for the first time since he'd started pacing, he went completely still. "And that has nothing to do with you being my mate," he added. "I was a lousy partner there."

The admission hung in the air, exposed and honest in a way that caught her completely off guard. She'd expected him to fall back on destiny and fate, to use the mate bond as an excuse for his change of heart. Instead, he was taking responsibility.

But she couldn't quite let go. "I'm playing the part of your mistress here, but that's not who I am. You said it yourself, your uncle is a godsdamned *king*. You can't just bring some former thief home and call it good. We can't—"

Strangely, Vex smiled. "You actually wouldn't be the first."

"What? You have other mates? I don't share." The vehemence in the words surprised her. But she'd had one taste of Vex, and she wasn't about to join some lord's harem just because he spoke prettily.

The thought of him with other women sent a spike of possessive fury through her that was completely irrational and absolutely undeniable. *He's mine*, something in her brain insisted, and the intensity of the feeling made her hands clench into fists.

He coughed and shook his head. "I mean that one of my cousins is mated to a former thief. She's human. They actually met when she tried to steal from him."

"You don't know me." The words came out smaller than she'd intended, carrying more vulnerability than she wanted to reveal.

He wouldn't be deterred. "And leaving you behind on Aetis won't exactly fix that. I'm not asking for vows of devotion on a week's acquaintance."

"It hasn't even been a week," she muttered.

Vex pointedly ignored that. "Come home to Vemion with me. Get to know me, the *real* me. Let's see what fate saw in the two of us. Give it a chance."

The offer was loaded with possibilities that

thrilled and terrified her. Home to Vemion. Home with *him*.

She wanted to say yes down to the tips of her toes. But Luisa had spent her life protecting herself, and she couldn't just give everything up for one rich man's promises.

Those were always fleeting.

"I have a job," she said. "The IDA hired me for a reason. I can't just take off and be your ... your ... *yours*. I'm not the kind of woman to sit around and do nothing, or whatever it is ladies do on your planet."

"They do whatever they want," he said dryly. Then he continued. "There's work for you on Vemion," he said. "I thought we worked well together, before it all went bad. And if you want to take your own jobs, I would never stop you." His voice carried absolute conviction, like the idea of controlling her choices was genuinely abhorrent to him.

"A month." The offer escaped before she could fully think it through, driven by hope and terror.

"What?" He went completely still.

"I'll give you a month. As a test run." She could use a vacation. And a dragon lord was practically kneeling at her feet, begging her to let him … love? … her.

When had anyone ever wanted her that desperately? When had anyone ever looked at her like she was something precious, something worth fighting for? The intensity in his gaze made her feel exposed and cherished.

She wasn't sure she could wrap her head around that.

But she could give him—and herself—a month.

The decision felt momentous and utterly terrifying, like stepping off the edge of a cliff with nothing but his promise to catch her.

It was the scariest thing she'd ever done in her life.

23

VEX HAD a month to convince his mate to stay with him forever, and he was wasting an afternoon at Zane's house.

He was a fool.

Twenty-six days. That's how much time he had left before Luisa would make her decision about whether their trial month was worth extending. The countdown felt like a sword hanging over his head, each passing hour bringing him closer to the moment when she would walk away forever.

He'd had Luisa on his estate for a week, and it was its own kind of torture. He'd asked her to come, to stay, to be his.

And now he had no idea how to *do* it.

He could negotiate trade agreements that affected entire star systems, could command respect from criminals and kings alike, could shift into a form that could level buildings with his fire.

But put him in a room with the woman fate had chosen for him, and he turned into a stammering fool who couldn't figure out how to bridge the careful distance she maintained between them.

If he'd truly been the playboy lord he'd pretended to be on Aetis, they would have spent every moment naked in bed. The dissolute rake would have seduced her with practiced ease, would have known exactly which words to whisper against her skin to make her melt in his arms.

But that man had been a mask, a performance designed to serve his mission. Now, faced with being himself, Vex felt like he was fumbling in the dark.

The most he'd done was hold her hand while they strolled through the garden.

The gentle getting to know you wasn't a waste. Vex cherished every moment at Luisa's side. He just wanted more of them.

All of them.

He wanted to wake up with her pressed against his chest every morning, wanted to know what she looked like when she was completely relaxed and unguarded. He wanted to hear her laugh without the careful edge she kept in her voice, wanted to see her eyes soften the way they had that one night when she'd let him hold her. The hunger for her was a constant ache, made worse by her proximity and the careful boundaries she maintained.

There was some sort of block between them, something they couldn't surmount.

It wasn't physical distance. They shared the same space, ate meals together, walked through his estate while she learned about his world. But there was an invisible wall between them, built from her past betrayals and his own uncertainty about how to be the man she needed.

Luisa was made of defensive walls. She'd opened up to him a bit one night, explained more of her childhood, of what had brought her into Brant Tallyer's orbit. He'd almost marched back to his ship and flown to Aetis to destroy the man.

His mate didn't cry. But she let him hold her.

The memory of that night was burned into his consciousness with perfect clarity. The way she'd curled against his chest on the library sofa, her voice steady and matter-of-fact as she'd described a childhood that would have broken most people. Hunger, abandonment, the desperate choices that survival demanded. She'd spoken like she was reciting someone else's history, but he'd felt the tremor in her hands where they'd gripped his shirt.

And in the morning, he had sent a note off to the concierge letting him know he would consider it a personal favor if Brant Tallyer was never employed again.

She'd grown up learning that powerful men were dangerous, that offers of protection came with prices she couldn't afford to pay. How could he convince her that he was different when every instinct screamed at him to claim her, possess her, keep her safe in ways that probably looked like cages to someone who'd fought so hard for her freedom?

If someone could help him overcome this block, maybe it was an *actual* playboy lord.

Zane.

His youngest brother had a reputation that was both legendary and completely deserved. Zane moved through relationships with the casual confidence of someone who'd never met a woman he couldn't charm.

Where Vex was all duty and restraint, Zane was pure hedonistic pleasure, living exactly the life their noble birth afforded him without the weight of responsibility.

Vex would never tell his brother that part of his dissolute rake version of Lord Vex was based on his youngest brother. It felt too much like an insult. Besides, neither Zane nor Rook knew exactly what it was that Vex did for the king, and he intended to keep it that way.

As far as Zane knew, Vex had met Luisa on a trip, and that was that.

Rook would hear the same, if he and his mate ever made it back to Vemion.

"You have that pretty human stashed away, why are you here?" Zane asked with a smirk as he joined Vex on the patio behind his home. The space was elegant granite fitted in intricate patterns, with comfortable seating arranged to take advantage of the spectacular valley view. Flowering vines filled the air with sweet perfume, the perfect place for entertaining. "Or do I finally get to meet her?"

Vex growled.

The sound rumbled from his chest before he could stop it, purely reflexive and completely reveal-ing. The thought of Zane meeting Luisa, of his charming brother turning that practiced smile on his mate, made smoke threaten to curl from his fingertips.

"Oh, it must be true love!" Zane laughed.

The delighted expression on his brother's face was insufferable. Zane looked like he'd just discovered the most entertaining secret in the galaxy, his eyes bright with mischief.

It could be. Maybe it was. Maybe it would be.

If he could figure out how to *touch* his mate.

"I can't visit my brother?" Vex asked.

"You can do anything you want. I don't see why you would though, when you have a beautiful woman—I'm assuming she's a beautiful woman—waiting for you back home." Zane's grin was pure wickedness.

"She had business to attend to," he said. "I thought I might visit."

"Business." Zane was doubtful.

She was on a call with her contact at the IDA filling them in on the data she'd found and what she'd destroyed. He couldn't tell Zane that.

Luisa's professional competence was one of the things he admired most about her, but it was also another barrier between them. She had a life, a career, responsibilities that existed completely independent of him. She didn't need him the way his dragon insisted she should.

"I don't think your mate should be able to *think* of business at this point in the relationship."

"How did you—I never said." With the looming threat of Luisa leaving at the end of the month, or sooner if she grew tired of him, Vex hadn't said a word to anyone of the true nature of their relationship.

He wanted to shout it from the skies.

But he was afraid.

Vex, who'd faced down armed criminals and negotiated with hostile governments, was terrified of a slip of a woman who barely reached his shoulder. Afraid she'd leave. Afraid she'd stay for the wrong reasons. Afraid he'd somehow damage the fragile trust they'd built by wanting too much, too fast.

He didn't know how to be afraid, and he certainly didn't like it.

"I've never seen you *dance* with a woman twice. Moving one into your home after a week-long vacation? You'd only do that with your mate." Zane looked insufferably pleased with his own deductive abilities. "Have you introduced her to Mother?"

"I haven't introduced her to anyone yet. She's not—we're not ... How?"

Zane's eyes widened, and his grin turned into an open-mouthed smile. "Surely you know ... *how*? Don't tell me—"

"Yes, I know *how.* Just because some dragons need to taste every woman that crosses their path doesn't mean the rest of us have ... insufficient needs."

"So what's the matter?" Zane leaned forward in his chair, suddenly serious despite the lingering amusement in his eyes.

"We met, and it was ..." Fiery. Passionate. Perfect.

A lie.

Every moment of their initial connection had been built on deception, on the roles they'd been playing for their mission. The dissolute lord and his pampered mistress had chemistry that could have set the casino on fire. But what did Vex of Vemion and Luisa of Aetis have? They were still figuring that out, still stumbling through the awkward process of learning who they really were when the masks came off.

He'd been playing a part. She'd been hiding

herself. Now they were exposed, and every move felt all the more real.

"The spark's left already?" Zane seemed doubtful.

"I want her more than anything." The words were ragged. "But I don't know ... how."

"Have you tried talking to her?" his brother asked, voice on the edge of sarcasm.

"All we do is talk!"

"Have you tried talking to her about sex?" Zane's expression was perfectly serious now, no trace of his earlier teasing. "Have you *had* sex with her?"

"Yes," Vex ground out through gritted teeth.

"And you can't do it again because ..."

Because the last time they'd fucked it had been to distract him from asking about her past.

The memory was a double-edged blade, cutting him with pleasure and pain in equal measure. Her mouth on his, her body welcoming him home, the way she'd whispered his name like a prayer. But underneath it all was the knowledge that she'd used their connection as a weapon, wielding her body to deflect questions she couldn't answer.

"If I met my mate, brother, I wouldn't let something as stupid as a lack of communication tear us apart. So, as surprising as this might sound, I think you need to go and *talk* to her. Or did you want to sit here and gossip all day?"

Vex glared and got up.

His chair scraped against the granite as he pushed back from the table. The sun was already starting to sink toward the horizon, painting the sky in shades that reminded him of Luisa's eyes when she was angry. He'd wasted enough time.

Little brothers were useless.

24

LUISA WAS ACTING RASHLY.

Not the first time.

But the stakes had never felt so high.

The past week at Vex's estate had been beautiful torture. Every morning brought shared breakfasts where his fingers would brush hers as he passed the fruit preserves, sending electricity up her arm.

Every afternoon meant long walks through his gardens where he'd take her hand to help her over uneven stone paths, his palm warm and calloused against her skin. Every evening ended with conversations that stretched deep into the night, sitting close enough on the library sofa that she could smell the smoke that always clung to his skin.

They'd talked about everything and nothing—

her childhood in the undercity, his responsibilities as a lord, the strange customs of different worlds they'd both visited. He listened to her stories without judgment, shared pieces of his own past that she suspected few people ever heard.

One night, they'd stayed up until sunrise. She'd curled against his side while he told her about learning to fly, and she'd felt more at home than she had anywhere in her life.

Despite all that the easy intimacy of their conversations, despite the way his eyes followed her every movement with barely contained hunger, he maintained a careful physical distance that was driving her slowly insane.

He looked at her like he was dying inside.

But he hadn't kissed her.

He hadn't done more than hold her hand.

She was about to explode with want.

The constant arousal was becoming a serious problem. She'd catch herself staring at his mouth when he spoke, remembering exactly how those lips had felt against her skin. The memory of his hands on her body haunted her dreams, leaving her to wake each morning aching and frustrated.

She was a big girl, and it was time to do something about that. Clearly, one of them had to be brave.

It felt a *tiny* bit unfair that as the human she had to be brave. He turned into a giant, fire breathing beast and could lob balls of flame at people without effort.

Which was maybe why he couldn't take the leap.

Dragons didn't have to be brave.

But humans who'd survived the undercity of Aetis? They knew how to take risks when the potential payoff was worth it. And Vex was worth every risk she could imagine taking.

Her outfit was a tiny bit out of character. Normally, to do what she was doing, she'd just wear something that would fit in … a staid suit, an evening gown, sturdy trousers, nothing to call attention.

She'd never thought to do it in a lacy skirt and sheer black top that hid *nothing*.

The fabric was gossamer-thin, so delicate it seemed like it might dissolve under a touch. The skirt barely qualified as clothing, more suggestion than coverage, and she'd forgone underwear entirely.

If this didn't get his attention, nothing would.

If this did work, she'd have to send a thank you note to whoever at the IDA had put together her mistress wardrobe.

Vex had an office that overlooked the forest. It was very conventional. A terminal at the desk, a dragon-proof safe bolted to the floor, a somewhat comfortable chair.

The space was purely functional, all clean lines and expensive materials. Afternoon sunlight streamed through the tall windows, casting geometric patterns across the dark wood floor.

And the *somewhat* comfortable chair was getting less comfortable by the second. She'd hacked his system forty-five minutes ago, and it should have set up an alarm. Really? What kind of security did the man have? She'd already made mental notes of what to fix.

If this worked.

It was going to work.

A shadow passed outside the window, a dragon landing behind the house.

Showtime.

Luisa had left the door open a crack. Vex always kept his office sealed shut. He hadn't forbidden her from entering. He'd even invited her to set up a workstation in there if she wanted.

She hadn't touched it.

Until today.

A few minutes later, Luisa heard footsteps on the stairs.

Her heart rate kicked up as the sound of his approach grew closer. This was it, no backing down now. She bent over the desk, fingers flying across the keyboard in a meaningless pattern that would look appropriately suspicious to anyone walking in.

Vex opened the door. "Hel—what are you doing?" He stopped dead in the doorway, his greeting cut off mid-word as he took in the scene before him.

Luisa shoved the keyboard away, eyes wide, and sat back in the chair.

Vex sucked in a ragged breath when he got a good look at her shirt. Or lack thereof.

Smoke began to curl around him as his eyes darkened, pupils dilating as he stared at her with draconic intensity. His nostrils flared, and she could see the exact moment his control began to slip. When he exhaled, wisps of smoke escaped his lips.

"What are you doing in here?" Vex repeated; it was nearly a growl.

"Nothing!" Luisa pushed back from the desk and stood and let him get an eye full of the skirt. It barely brushed the edge of her ass. "You definitely didn't just catch a hacker trying to infiltrate your system." She paused and waited.

He stepped fully into the room and closed the door behind him with calculated precision, the soft click of the lock engaging somehow managing to sound both promising and threatening.

"I didn't?" he asked. "Then what are you doing at my desk? At my computer? Do you know what I do to people who try and take advantage?" He moved closer, each step measured, closing the distance between them.

I sure hope so, she thought.

"You've got it all wrong," she breathed. "Is there anything I can do to make you understand?" She traced her hand across her stomach, just under her breasts.

Vex's nostrils flared, and he breathed out smoke.

"I was coming to talk to you, you know," he said.

"Haven't we done enough talking?" She was so sick of talking she was ready to tape her mouth shut … or find another use for it.

He grinned and swaggered forward, and for a second, he was the Lord Vex from Aetis all over again. But Luisa saw through it. It wasn't the act.

No, this was *her* Vex.

He was just allowing himself to have fun.

"On the desk," he commanded.

Luisa perched on the edge of the polished wood surface, hands folded primly in her lap and knees pressed together with an innocence that was completely at odds with her scandalous outfit.

Vex stalked closer until he stood directly in front of her, close enough that she could feel the heat radiating from his skin but not quite touching. His scent surrounded her—smoke and cedar that made her mouth water with want.

"Let's see what you've taken from me." He traced a hand down the sheer fabric of her arm. Then his fingers curled into the sleeve, and he tugged.

It tore away like tissue.

The delicate material parted with barely any resistance, leaving her right shoulder and arm completely bare. Vex's eyes followed the path of exposed skin with ravenous attention. He reached for the other sleeve, this time gripping it with both hands and pulling until the entire top came away in tatters, leaving her naked from the waist up.

"Looking for contraband," he murmured, his voice rough with barely contained desire as his hands came up to cup her breasts. His palms were furnace-hot against her sensitive skin, and she couldn't suppress the soft moan that escaped her lips as his thumbs brushed over her already-tight nipples.

His mouth followed the path his hands had taken, lips and tongue lavishing attention on the curve of her breasts before he drew one nipple into his mouth. The sensation shot straight to her core, making her arch against him as he sucked and nibbled with devastating skill.

"Nothing there," Vex murmured, kissing her breasts once more. "Open your legs." The command was ragged.

Luisa's legs fell open.

Vex's hands settled on her inner thighs, his touch gentle but possessive as he traced patterns on the sensitive skin. His fingers moved higher with agonizing slowness, teasing closer and closer to where she needed him most. When he discovered her lack of underwear, his breath hissed out between his teeth.

"Such a naughty thief," he growled, his voice thick with approval and desire. "Coming into my office dressed like this, with nothing underneath." His fingers stroked along the outside of her sex, barely touching but enough to make her hips jerk toward him involuntarily.

When he finally slipped two fingers inside her, she cried out at the sudden fullness, her inner walls clenching around the welcome intrusion. He worked her with precision, his thumb finding that sensitive bundle of nerves while his fingers moved in a rhythm that had her writhing against the desk.

"So wet," he said. "Do you get off on stealing from people?"

"Only you." It was so, so true.

He increased the pace of his fingers, curling them in a way that hit that perfect spot inside her. When her orgasm finally hit, it tore through her with devastating force, leaving her crying out his name as her body convulsed around his fingers.

Before she had time to recover, she heard the sound of fabric rustling as he freed himself from his trousers. Then he was positioning himself between her thighs, the thick head of his cock nudging against her entrance.

He thrust forward in one smooth motion, filling her completely and drawing a moan from both of them at the perfect fit.

Finally, she could touch him. Her arms came up to wrap around his shoulders, pulling him closer as he began to move inside her. The feel of him was everything she'd been craving during their week of careful distance—the solid weight of his body against hers, the stretch and fullness as he claimed her.

Her second orgasm built more slowly this time, a deep, rolling wave that seemed to start in her very core and spread outward until every nerve was singing with pleasure. When it finally crested, it pulled him over the edge with her, his movements becoming erratic as he spilled himself inside her with a groan that she felt as much as heard.

Vex collapsed back into the chair, pulling a mostly limp and sated Luisa with him. She was a ragdoll, too full of pleasure to do more than slump over him.

"Did you want to talk about something?" Luisa asked sometime later, her lips moving against his shirt.

He was still wearing most of his clothes.

That was a problem. But she wasn't about to move to solve it.

"We can talk about it in bed," he said.

And without giving her time to respond, he picked her up and carried her out of the office.

NEED A LITTLE MORE OF VEX & LUISA?

Sign up at the link below to **receive a free bonus epilogue!**

Get your free bonus epilogue!

https://katerudolph.net/index.php/vex-bonus/

————

Thank you so much for reading *Rook*!
Your support means the world to me. If you enjoyed the story, it would mean even more if you could take a moment to share your thoughts in a review or leave a rating.
Hearing from readers like you makes all the difference!

————

The Dragon Brides series continues with Zane!

————

WHAT TO READ NEXT: ZANE

He's the playboy dragon lord. She's the one gamble he can't walk away from.

Dragon Lord Zane has everything: looks, power, charm, and a reputation for never taking anything seriously. The only thing he won't risk? His freedom. He's seen what an unhappy match can do to a dragon, and he refuses to be chained. One night with a mysterious card sharp should have been nothing but fun… until he wakes up alone, craving more.

Mercy Webb knows better than to trust rich, powerful men, especially the gorgeous dragon who ruined her focus at the table and in her bed. With her grandmother's life on the line, she signs up for Planet of Desire, the galaxy's most scandalous dating show.

Win the prize money. Save her family. Simple.

Until Zane walks on stage.

Now they're forced together for the cameras, trapped in dangerous challenges that test more than survival. Every look sparks heat. Every touch threatens to burn.

She swore she'd never be owned. He swore he'd never surrender.

But the mate bond doesn't care.

And on Ofros, the only thing more dangerous than the predators outside… is the fire they ignite inside each other.

Read today!

He is the scandalous lord no one takes seriously, and he's determined to keep it that way…

Zane's plan is simple: sabotage his own royal matchmaking by vanishing for a week. All it takes is a few reckless smiles, a little mischief, and a quick getaway with jaded cargo pilot Mercy Webb, who's willing to haul him to the farthest edge of the sector. Perfect.

No obligations. No scrutiny. No strings.

Until pirates storm their ship and turn his simple game into a fight for survival.

Mercy has no patience for spoiled nobles or the trouble they cause. She survives on grit, skill, and never letting anyone close, not after what her father's legacy cost her. All she wants is enough credits to keep her ship in the sky.

Instead, she is stuck with Zane: too pretty, too curious, and far too tempting.

Now survival means working together to outwit ruthless pirates and navigate the wildfire chemistry sparking between them. To win this fight, they must risk the one thing they both swore never to give again: trust.

LOOKING for love that's out of this world? These strong, smart, sexy aliens are seeking mates from the Milky Way. Just hop onboard with your local Intergalactic Dating Agency. Join our group of authors as we explore the friendly skies and beyond with trilogies of cosmic craving, astral adventure, and otherworldly lovers. Warning: abductions may or may not be included!

Dragon Brides
Dragon Princes. Fierce Women. Love.
Fated mates, fierce women, and dragon princes are ready to find their mates.

Crux

Ranger

Saber

Cipher

Storm

Drake

Asher

Knox

Flint

Pine

Rook
Vex
Zane

Drakarn Mates

A harsh desert planet. Stranded humans. Draconic aliens. A match made in… well, somewhere.

Claimed by the Drakarn Warrior Lord
Echoes of Fire
Scorched by Fate
Fated to the Drakarn Commander
Chained to the Champion
Beast of Blood and Ash

Guarded by the Shifter

Werewolf. Bodyguard. Mate.

The origins of these shifters are shrouded in mystery, but they're determined to protect their mates from any harm that comes their way.

Also available in audio!
Hunting Season
On the Prowl
Stalking Magic
Hungry for the Wolf
Wolf Cursed (novella)
Wolf's Temptation

———

Stealing the Alpha

The thief takes what she wants, but the alpha keeps what's his...

Join shifter thief Mel as she clashes with lion alpha Luke in an explosive trilogy of two opposites who can't keep away from one another.

Also available in audio!
The Alpha Heist
Entangled with the Thief
In the Alpha's Bed

———

Alien Mates: Planet Exile

Guerran is no place for pretty human women. But these alien heroes will protect their mates!
Also available in audio!

Exile's Hunter
Exile's Adored

———

Zulir Warrior Mates

Kidnapped humans. Alien Warriors. Electric wings.
The Zulir Warrior Mates series brings you human heroines and heroes abducted from Earth who find love – and wings! – with the alien warriors who rescue them.
Also available in audio!

Synnr's Saint
Synnr's Hope
Synnr's Spark
Synnr's Kiss
Synnr's Ride

———

Mated to the Alien

Fated Mate Alien Romance

Detyens are doomed to die young if they don't find their fated mates.

Follow along as these mated pairs fight off aliens, corrupt dictators, prejudiced humans, pirates, and more! The books can be read or listened to in any order, though some characters show up in multiple stories.

Select books available in audio.

Pick a book and jump into the action today!

Ruwen

Tyral

Stoan

Cyborg

Krayter

Kayleb

Shayn

Braxtyn

Doryan

Dekon

———

Detyen Warriors

Detya was destroyed a hundred years ago. These doomed warriors are out to find justice… and their mates.

The Detyen Warriors series brings you kick butt heroines, alpha alien heroes, fated mates, and relationships strong enough to span the galaxy!

The entire series is also available in audio!

Soulless

Ruthless

Heartless

Faultless

Endless

Detyen Warrior Outcasts
Fated Mate Alien Romance

These doomed warriors were abandoned by their people and live on the edge. Their mates hold the key to their salvation.

Pick a book and jump into the action today!

Dangerous Bond

Intrepid Bond

Wayward Bond

Alien Holiday Romance

Christmas… in space????
These alien holiday romances look beyond Earth's winter holidays and ring in the season across the galaxy!
Select titles available in audio.
Snowed in with the Alien Beast
The Alien's Winter Gift
The Alien Reindeer's Wild Ride
Trapped with her Alien Mate

Alien Outlaws

Outlaws, schemes, and love… it's all there in the Alien Outlaws series…
Andie Munster is sick of life on Ixilta, the planet she got dumped on after being abducted from Earth six years ago. And when the mysterious and dangerous Xandr shows up looking for a way off the planet, she's half-prisoner, half-co-conspirator in a wild rush to escape.

Rogue Alien's Escape
Rogue Alien's Woman
Rogue Alien's Secret
Rogue Alien's Legacy

Find more by Kate Rudolph at www.
katerudolph.net

ABOUT KATE RUDOLPH

KATE RUDOLPH IS a paranormal and sci-fi romance writer who lives in Indiana. She loves writing about kick butt heroines and the steamy heroes who love them. She's been devouring romance novels since she was too young to be reading them and had to hide her books so no one would take them away. She couldn't imagine a better job in this world than writing romances and sharing them with her fellow readers.

If you enjoyed this story, please consider leaving a review.